*Mary June said she would come and get me,* Kristy thought as she poured quarter after quarter into the video machine. *I'll just play until I get to level five.*

Instead, Kristy played until she ran out of money. She glanced down at her watch. "One-thirty!" she gasped. What had happened to Mary June?

Running out into the lobby, Kristy took the elevator to the thirtieth floor. In front of her door, she remembered that she had no key. Her heart beating fast, she knocked softly.

"Mary June!" she whispered. "Mary June! It's me! Open up!"

The door clicked open. Mrs. Williams was standing there in her nightgown.

"Kristy, what on earth are you doing out in the hall?" she said crossly, rubbing her eyes. "You're supposed to be in bed. Don't wake Mary June."

Kristy crept into the room and changed into her pajamas in the bathroom. She glanced at herself in the mirror with a guilty expression. She knew that what she had done was wrong. If the coach found out, he would be angry. He might even pull her from Junior Olympics!

Be sure to read all the exciting
AMERICAN GOLD SWIMMERS
titles from Bantam Books:

# AMERICAN GOLD SWIMMERS

# The HUMAN SHARK

## SHARON DENNIS WYETH

**BANTAM BOOKS**

New York · Toronto · London · Sydney · Auckland

*RL 4.5, 008–012*
*THE HUMAN SHARK*
*A Bantam Skylark Book / June 1996*

*Skylark Books is a registered trademark of Bantam Books,*
*a division of Bantam Doubleday Dell Publishing Group, Inc.*
*Registered in the U.S. Patent and Trademark Office and elsewhere.*

*Series cover design: Madalina Stefan*

ISBN 0-553-48395-1

*Published simultaneously in the United States and Canada*

*Bantam Books are published by Bantam Books, a division of Bantam Doubleday Dell Publishing Group, Inc. Its trademark, consisting of the words "Bantam Books" and the portrayal of a rooster, is Registered in U.S. Patent and Trademark Office and in other countries. Marca Registrada. Bantam Books, 1540 Broadway, New York, New York 10036.*

PRINTED IN THE UNITED STATES OF AMERICA

OPM   0   9   8   7   6   5   4   3   2   1

*For Brian Reich and Leslie Kotin*

# ONE

### "NUCLEAR ADAMS" SET TO EXPLODE AT JUNIOR OLYMPICS

by Charles Flowers
*Special to The Surfside Gazette*

Kirk and Kristy Adams, the brother-and-sister swimming pair nicknamed "the Nuclear Adams" because of their explosive swimming styles, will compete at the Junior Olympics next weekend in Fort Lauderdale.

Fourteen-year-old Kirk has already set records this year in two butterfly events. Twelve-year-old Kristy has set a record in the freestyle.

The brother and sister will swim for their club team, the Aquatic Dolphins, based here in Surfside. Along with other members of the team, Kirk and Kristy have been practicing up to 25 hours a week to prepare for the Junior Olympics.

"I'm putting everything I've got into this J.O.," said Kirk, who is a baby-faced barracuda in the water. His sister, Kristy, is an aggressive competitor too. The lanky 12-year-old may look like a mermaid, but in the water, she's a shark.

"Kristy! Open up! Are you in there? It's me—Rosa!"

Kristy Adams flung open the door of her room. Her suitcase was on the bed, and clothes were hanging out of her dresser drawers.

"Rosie!" She threw her arms around Rosa Gonzalez, her best friend. "You're just in time to help me. What are you doing here, anyway? You're supposed to be in school."

"You're not the only one who got to leave early today," Rosa said with a wide grin. "Aren't you and Kirk leaving soon? I thought you'd be packed."

Kristy looked at the open suitcase and threw up her hands. "I've been trying to pack for an hour, but I keep changing my mind about what to bring. I've never been in a Junior Olympics. What should I wear?"

"Bathing suits," said Rosa, plopping down into Kristy's pink armchair.

"Oh, I've got five of those packed," said Kristy.

Rosa raised her eyebrows. "Five? You're only going to be there Friday, Saturday, and Sunday."

"But on Saturday I'm swimming in two sessions," Kristy said, tossing a pair of white cutoffs onto the bed. "I have two team suits and two old drag suits for practice."

Rosa fiddled with the bright red tie that held back her long, dark hair. "What's the fifth swimsuit for?"

"In case we go to the beach, of course," Kristy said.

"The beach!" exclaimed Rosa. "I didn't know we were going to the beach!"

Kristy looked at her in surprise. "We? But you're not—"

Rosa smiled. "I've got a surprise for you. That's why I'm here. Coach Reich called my mother and—"

Rosa was interrupted by a voice in the hall.

"Ouch! C'mon, Kristy! Can't you keep your suitcase out of the way? I almost broke my toe!"

Kristy ran to the door of her room.

"Uh-oh," said Rosa.

Kirk Adams stood at the top of the stairs, hopping around on one foot. An oversized brown suitcase sat in the middle of the hallway.

"Your suitcase could have broken my toe," said Kirk. "If I have to miss the J.O. because of—"

"You're always blaming stuff on me," snapped Kristy. "For your information, that isn't my suitcase."

Kirk dropped his foot. "Oh. Whose is it, then?"

"How should I know?" Kristy said. She bent down to look at her brother's foot. Her long, light brown hair fell over one eye. "Take your shoe off," she said, brushing her hair out of her face.

"Never mind," said Kirk. "There's no time for you to play doctor. I bet you're not even packed yet."

"She's almost packed," Rosa said, waltzing into the hall. "About this," she said, lugging the suitcase to one side. "It's mine."

Kristy's eyes lit up. "Yours?"

"Yes," said Rosa, "that's what I was about to tell you. Coach Reich called my mother and father and asked if I wanted to be a coach's assistant. Coach Apple recommended me because I did a good job as her assistant on the school team. So even though I'm not going to compete, I'm going to the Junior Olympics too."

"Great!" said Kristy. She grabbed Rosa's hands and pulled her back into the room. "We're going to have such a good time! Now, help me finish packing or my mother will kill me."

"Hey, Rosa," Kirk said. He stood in Kristy's doorway.

Rosa blushed. "What is it, Kirk?"

Kirk stuck his hands in his pockets. "Sorry I yelled about the suitcase. I didn't know it was yours."

"He only yells at me," said Kristy.

"Oh, it's all right," said Rosa, looking down at the floor. "I hope your pinky toe isn't too crushed."

"It's fine," Kirk said, backing up. "I'm glad you're coming to J.O. too," he said, and dashed away.

"I thought you said you didn't like-like Kirk anymore," Kristy said, tossing a pair of sandals into her suitcase.

Rosa looked at herself in the mirror. "I thought I didn't."

"You said you like-liked Jonah," Kristy reminded her.

Rosa threw up her hands. "Jonah and Kirk are so different," she said. "I think I like-like them both. You know?"

"Not really," Kristy said. Poking around in the suitcase, she came up with a pair of goggles and tucked them back in again. "I thought I packed an extra pair of these."

"Need any help?" asked Rosa.

"The checklist is on the dresser," Kristy said. "Read it off. I've been packing for so long, I don't remember what's in here."

Rosa picked up the list. "Okay, here goes. Two team suits, team cap, three extra suits, two pairs goggles—"

"Check," Kristy said, rummaging through the things in her bag.

"Three towels, a sweatshirt, three pairs of shorts, three T-shirts, sneakers, pajamas, water shoes, water bottle, healthy snacks, toilet articles, sleeping bag. That's it."

"Got it," Kristy said. "All except the snacks. Mom has those in the cooler downstairs along with the sleeping bags." She tugged the suitcase onto the floor and sat on it.

"You've got a lot more than that in there," Rosa said, eyeing the suitcase. "That thing is so full, you can't even close it."

"You're right," Kristy said, struggling to mash down the top. "I can't."

"Get up," Rosa said. "Let me look in there."

Kristy got up. Rosa bent over the suitcase and pulled out a pair of boots. "What are these for? You're not going fishing."

"I thought it might rain," explained Kristy.

Rosa tossed the boots toward the closet. "Out!"

There was a knock at the door. "How are you doing in there, Princess?" Kristy's father appeared in the doorway. He was wearing a cowboy hat with his cardigan and slacks.

"Okay, Dad," Kristy said. "Except that I can't close my suitcase."

"Maybe you should sit on it, Mr. Adams," Rosa suggested. "By the way, your hat is cool."

"Thanks," Mr. Adams said, sitting on the suitcase. "I couldn't resist trying it on. It's one of the costumes for the play we're opening this weekend at the college—the musical *Oklahoma!*" Mr. Adams was a drama professor at the college in Surfside.

The suitcase snapped shut. "Now all you need is your shoes," Mr. Adams said, noticing Kristy's bare feet.

"Uh-oh," said Kristy. "I think I packed them."

Rosa giggled.

"We can't have you going barefoot to Junior Olympics," Mr. Adams said, reopening the suitcase and taking out Kristy's sneakers. "Mermaids have fish tails, not bare feet."

"Don't mention mermaids," Kristy said, stuffing her feet into her shoes. "That's what that guy called me in the newspaper."

Mr. Adams winked at Rosa. "She hates publicity."

"He also called me a shark," Kristy complained, trudging out of her room with the suitcase.

"I'd think it was awesome if somebody wrote about me in the paper," said Rosa, trotting behind her. "Besides, I'm sure that when that reporter called you a shark, he meant it as a compliment."

"Even if he did," Kristy said, dropping her bag, "I don't like it. I'm not a shark *or* a mermaid. I'm just normal. Besides, having thousands of people read about me in the paper is nerve-racking."

"I'll take your suitcase downstairs," said Mr. Adams. "Then I'll come back for Rosa's."

"That's okay," said Rosa, picking up her big bag. "I can do it."

Kirk zipped up the stairs past Kristy. "Please, Rosa," he said, grabbing the suitcase from her. "Let me do it."

"Thanks," Rosa said, blushing again. "That's very polite, especially for a baby-faced barracuda."

"Did you read that article?" Kirk said eagerly. "That reporter really likes us."

"What a publicity hog," said Kristy.

"Come and get it," Dr. Adams called from the foot of the stairs. "I've made some lunch. Shrimp and macaroni salad."

"Way to go, Mom! My favorite!" shouted Kirk as they filed downstairs.

"I'll take the suitcases out to the car," said Mr. Adams. "You guys go eat."

Kristy, Rosa, and Kirk went into the kitchen. Hamlet, the older of the two family dogs, lay stretched in front of the sink, taking a nap. But their fuzzy black puppy, Sylvia, ran over to meet them.

"Hi, Sylvia," Kristy said, kneeling down so that the dog could lick her face. "Since you're a Portuguese water dog, you'd probably do well in Junior Olympics."

Dr. Adams chuckled. "An Olympics for dogs. I'm sure someone will come up with it."

"It would be great for you, Mom," said Kirk. "You're already a veterinarian. You could specialize in sports medicine for dogs and make a bundle of money."

"You could enter Sylvia in the dog Olympics, too," Rosa suggested.

Kristy laughed. "And we could all go see her."

Dr. Adams laughed and served up three plates. "I just wish I could see you in Junior Olympics," she said. "This will be the first time your father and I have missed it." She put Kristy's plate in front of her. "I feel especially sorry to miss you, sweetheart," she said. She gave Kristy's hair a pat. "After all, Kirk has swum in Junior Olympics before. This will be your first time."

"That's okay, Mom," Kristy said, popping a big piece of shrimp into her mouth. "I know Grandma's sick and that you have to take care of her."

"And we know that Dad has to be there when his drama students open in their play," Kirk said, wolfing down his macaroni salad.

Kirk and Kristy ate with gusto, while Rosa picked at her food.

"Rosa, don't you like the shrimp?" asked Dr. Adams.

"I love it," said Rosa, "but I'm not very hungry. My mother left me some rice and beans for lunch."

"Yum," said Kristy. "I love Mrs. Gonzalez's rice and beans."

"Got enough carbos, Kirk?" asked Dr. Adams as Kirk got up from the table. "Or do you want another helping of macaroni salad?"

"I'm done," Kirk said, opening a small cooler on the counter. "Hmm, maybe I will have a granola bar."

"Get one from the cupboard," Dr. Adams said. "I've packed those for you and Kristy to take to the meets. Of course, you're welcome to have some of those snacks too, Rosa."

"Thanks, Dr. Adams," said Rosa. "It's really nice of you and Mr. Adams to drive me to the bus. My mother would have done it, but she's working."

Kirk got a box of granola bars out of the cupboard and held it out to Rosa. "Have one?"

"No thanks," said Rosa.

"How about me?" Kristy said, reaching into the box. "Or am I invisible?"

Kirk rolled his eyes. "Of course you're not."

Mr. Adams came into the kitchen. "Let's go. We've got about fifteen minutes to get to the bus."

Everybody jumped up. "Oh, kids," said Dr. Adams, grabbing the cooler. "I feel so awful that I'm not going." She gave Kirk a kiss. "I'll say good-bye now, so that you won't be embarrassed at the bus."

"Aw, Mom," Kirk said, wiping his cheek.

"Good luck," Dr. Adams said, hugging Kristy.

"She doesn't need any luck," Mr. Adams said, patting Kristy on the back. "She's worked hard. And if she gets a medal at Junior Olympics, it'll be because she earned it."

"Thanks, Dad," Kristy said, feeling a flutter in her stomach. "But talking about medals just makes me nervous."

"All right," said Mr. Adams, giving her a kiss on the cheek. "We won't talk about it."

Dr. Adams hugged Rosa. "I'm sure you'll be a great help to Coach Reich."

Rosa smiled. "Thanks, Dr. Adams."

"Can we get done with the mushy stuff?" Kirk asked, opening the door. "We've got a bus to catch."

"Righto," said Dr. Adams.

Rosa and the Adamses got into the station wagon. Sylvia hopped in and sat on one of the suitcases.

Kirk reached into his pocket and took out a deck of cards. "Whew," he said. "I thought I'd forgotten these. I'm rooming with Jonah, and he loves to play I Doubt It."

"Is Jonah's dad going to chaperone?" asked Dr. Adams.

"Yes, Mr. Walsh is coming," Kirk replied, leaning forward in his seat. "The kids whose parents aren't coming will be rooming with kids whose parents are coming. That way there'll be enough chaperones."

"I wonder who I'll be rooming with," said Rosa.

"With me," said Kristy.

"But my mom isn't coming," said Rosa. "And the coach just invited me last night. The roommate assignments were probably made days ago."

"Well, we'll just ask him to switch them," Kristy said, twisting around to pet Sylvia. "If my best friend is going on a trip with me, we have to be roommates. And that's that."

"If Rosa isn't your roommate, don't make a big thing out of it," said Kirk.

"Why not?" said Kristy.

"Coach Reich has got a million things to organize for the meet," Kirk explained. "I know from experience that he doesn't like complainers. Especially about little things like roommates."

"Maybe if Kristy asks him politely," said Dr. Adams, turning around, "the coach won't mind trying to work it out."

"I just wouldn't fuss too much," Kirk warned. "After all, there are fifty swimmers on the team. They all can't room with their first choice."

The car rounded the bend to the Aquatic Dolphins Club and pulled into the palm-lined driveway. Kids and their parents were lining up to board a big gray bus.

"Don't wander around in the hotel alone," said Mr. Adams, jumping out of the car. "Don't pig out on junk food."

"Don't talk to strangers in the elevator," said Dr. Adams, grabbing the two rolled-up sleeping bags Kirk and Kristy would sit on at the competition.

"Not even a reporter?" asked Kirk, picking up his suitcase.

"Especially not a reporter," Kristy murmured. She gave Sylvia a last-minute pat.

A short boy with deep brown skin and sparkling brown eyes ran up to the car.

"Morning, everybody," he said with a smile.

"Morning, Jonah," said Dr. Adams.

Jonah slapped Kirk's hand. "Bring the cards, Holier-than-Thou?"

Rosa giggled. "Holier-than-Thou . . ."

"He calls Kirk that because of all the holes in his practice suit," Kristy explained to her father.

Mr. Adams laughed. "Let's go, troops," he said, taking Kristy's suitcase and the cooler in one hand and Rosa's suitcase in the other.

Kristy's heart pounded with excitement as she jogged toward the bus. She'd been to Junior Olympics before, but always to see Kirk. She'd never thought she'd be a participant. It seemed as if it had been only a couple of months ago that she'd tried out for the middle-school swim team, the Surfside Waves. Now she was not only a member of the Waves, but also a member of the Aquatic Dolphins. She had already set a record in the freestyle at an area championship meet.

Her mother gave her one last hug. "I'll miss you, Kristy," she whispered.

Kristy felt a lump in her throat. Suddenly three days seemed like three months. "I wish you could come," she said.

"I'll call you," Dr. Adams promised, giving Kristy's arm a squeeze.

"Break a fin," said Mr. Adams, hugging Kristy's shoulders.

"I'll do my best," Kristy promised.

Coach Reich was standing next to the bus, holding a clipboard. The wind had tousled the thick brown hair around his bald spot.

"Morning, Kristy," said the coach with a nod. "I've got you checked in. You can get on."

"Here are some snacks for the bus," Dr. Adams said, thrusting a brown bag into Kristy's hand. "For you and Kirk to share with your teammates."

"Thanks, Mom," Kirk said, pushing ahead with Jonah.

"Good-bye, Dr. Adams," Rosa said, climbing up after them.

Mr. Adams waved from where he was stowing the suitcases, sleeping bags, and cooler in the luggage compartment of the bus.

Kristy waved and then faced Coach Reich.

"You can get on," said the coach.

"Okay," said Kristy. "But first, could you please tell me who my roommate is? I hope it's Rosa Gonzalez."

"Let me see . . . ," the coach mumbled, checking his list. "It's not Rosa," he said. "It's Mary June Williams."

Kristy's mouth dropped open. "Mary June Williams?"

"The only Mary June on our team," said the coach. "Don't you know her?"

Kristy nodded. She knew Mary June, all right. Mary June was a very good swimmer, but she was also very competitive and very boastful. Not only that, but Kristy was sure Mary June hated her.

"Can I make a switch?" Kristy asked, clutching the coach's arm.

"Please get on the bus, Kristy," the coach said. "I can't discuss this now." He glanced back over his shoulder, and Kristy followed his gaze. Mary June and her mother were standing there. They were both blond and tall.

"Could we move along?" Mrs. Williams said, cocking her head.

"Hi, Kristy," said Mary June. "I read that piece in the newspaper where the reporter called you a shark." She batted her big blue eyes. "It was perfect."

Kristy turned around and got on the bus. Five minutes before, going to Junior Olympics had seemed perfect too. But now, with Mary June Williams as her roommate, who could tell what it would be like?

# TWO

Rosa was sitting at the front of the bus. "I saved a seat for you," she told Kristy.

"Thanks for picking seats in the front," Kristy said, slipping in beside her. "A front seat is best for me because I get carsick."

The bus's engine began to hum as the last arrivals boarded. Kristy looked across Rosa and out the window. Her parents waved at her and Kirk.

Kristy felt someone bump her shoulder. It was Mrs. Williams, putting her tote bag in the overhead rack. Kristy looked up at her.

"Would you mind switching seats with us?" Mrs. Williams asked, peering down. "The chaperones have to sit near the front."

Rosa jumped up quickly and bumped her head. "Ouch. Oh, sure, Mrs. Williams."

"Take your seats, please," Coach Reich said, leaning across the aisle.

"Sorry, Coach," chirped Mrs. Williams. Mary June

hung on to the back of the seat as the bus lurched forward.

"Would you mind, Kristy?" Mary June asked. "I'd really like to sit with my mother."

Kristy half stood. The bus turned, and Rosa clung to Kristy's back to keep from falling.

"Steady, girls," Coach Reich said, getting up from his seat. "Please let Mrs. Williams have the two front seats and move back."

"Sure, Coach," said Kristy.

Kristy and Rosa walked down the aisle, holding on to the seat handles to steady themselves. Even though they'd just left the parking lot, the bus was already noisy.

"There goes my stomach," Kristy said as the bus made another turn.

"Once we get on the highway, I'm sure the ride will be much smoother," said Rosa. The girls took seats in the middle of the bus, across the aisle from Kirk and Jonah.

"Too bad we had to give away the front seat," said Rosa.

"I'll be okay," said Kristy, pressing her face to the window. "I suppose it was only right that we give the seats to Mrs. Williams, since she's a chaperone."

"I've got a deck of cards," Kirk said, leaning across the aisle. "Want to play I Doubt It, Rosa?"

"I'm up for it," said Rosa. "I'm pretty good at that game."

"After you beat Kirk, you can play me," Jonah said from his seat.

"What makes you think she's going to beat me?" Kirk asked.

Jonah grinned. "*I* always beat you."

"Well, maybe you and I should play first," Kirk said.

"Let's do it," said Jonah. "And the loser has to pay for the first round of video games."

"Am I playing or not?" Rosa asked. The boys looked at each other. "I guess the answer to that is 'I doubt it,' " said Rosa, answering her own question.

"You can play the winner," said Jonah. "And I *doubt* that it will be Kirk."

"Deal the cards," Kirk said, handing Jonah the deck. "We'll see."

Reaching into the bag her mother had packed, Kristy pulled out a candy bar.

"You should save that for later," warned Kirk.

Kristy bit into the candy. "My sweet tooth doubts that your opinion matters."

Jonah and Rosa giggled.

"You should pay attention to your cards," Rosa suggested to Kirk, "or you'll end up paying for all the video games."

"What's all this about video games?" Kristy asked, licking chocolate off her finger.

"The hotel probably has an arcade," said Jonah. "Most of them do."

"Neat," said Kristy. "I only brought twenty-five dollars with me. I hope that's enough."

"T-Twenty-five dollars!" Kirk sputtered, looking up from his cards. "You'd have to play video games all night long to spend that much money. You're going to have to go to bed pretty early."

"Says who?" said Kristy.

"Says your big brother," teased Rosa. "You know how he likes to keep an eye on you."

"Do I ever," grumbled Kristy.

"Four aces," Jonah said, hugging his cards to his chest. "Do you believe me or not?"

Kirk sneaked a look at his own cards. "I doubt it," he said.

Jonah laughed and showed his cards. "You got me," he said. "I only have two sixes and two fours."

Kirk took the cards and shuffled them. "Now you and I have to play," he said, smiling at Rosa.

Rosa's eyes sparkled. "Fine. But I doubt that you'll beat me."

Kristy reached into her bag again. "Want some gum?" she asked.

"I do," said a voice from the seat behind her. Kristy turned around. Donna O'Brien was sitting there, holding her hand out.

"Are you sure?" Kristy asked. "Won't it get stuck in your braces?"

Donna smiled, revealing a mouthful of metal. "I don't really chew it," she confessed. "I just suck on it."

"Be my guest," Kristy said, dropping a stick of gum into Donna's hand. "Just let me know if you need more. My mom packed me tons on account of my motion sickness."

"Thanks," said Donna, peeling the wrapper back. "By the way, Rosa," she said, tapping the seat, "we're roommates."

"Really?" Rosa said. As she turned around, her cards tipped forward.

"Hold on to your cards," warned Kirk. "I might sneak a peek at them."

"I doubt it," said Rosa, retrieving a card from the floor. "You're much too honest for that."

Kristy turned around in her seat to face Donna. "Is Rosa really your roommate?" she asked.

Donna nodded. "We got a call last night."

"Who's your chaperone?" Kristy asked.

"My mother," Donna said. "She's sitting up front."

"Lucky you." Kristy sighed. "I wish I could room with Rosa."

"Who's your roommate?" Donna asked.

Kristy made a face. "Mary June."

Donna grinned. "That should be interesting."

"Did you say you were rooming with Mary June?" Rosa asked, tugging Kristy's arm.

"Yes." Kristy sighed. "I wish I could switch so that you and I could room together."

"Ready?" Kirk asked, waving his cards to get Rosa's attention. "Do you want me to go first?"

"No, I'll go first," said Rosa. She held her cards to her chest. "Three queens."

Kirk shook his head. "I doubt it."

"Eat your heart out," said Rosa, showing her cards.

"Wow," said Jonah. "She beat you."

Kristy gazed out the window for a minute. The bus whizzed by palm trees blowing in the breeze, a couple of motels, and a mall.

"To think I'm going to stay in a fancy hotel with a video arcade and I'm stuck with Mary June as my roommate," muttered Kristy.

"Try to make the best of it," said Kirk.

"I doubt it," said Kristy. "I'm going to switch."

"I doubt that anyone will want to switch," Donna piped up. "She's not too popular."

"That's why Kristy ought to be a good sport about it," Kirk said, giving his sister a look.

Kristy wondered what Kirk meant.

Coach Reich walked halfway down the aisle. "How are we doing back here?"

"Okay, Coach," Kirk said.

"How about you girls?" he asked, looking over at Rosa and Kristy. "Your mother told me that you have a tendency to get motion sickness, Kristy."

"My stomach is holding out so far," said Kristy.

"Is it true that you competed in the Olympics?" Rosa asked.

Coach Reich nodded. "Almost. I was scheduled to compete with the U.S. team in 1966. But we boycotted because of a political situation."

"You must have been so disappointed," said Kristy.

"I was," said the coach. "But I stood by the committee's decision. And I've always been proud that I was chosen for an Olympic team."

Coach Reich peeked at Jonah's hand. "Better fold."

Jonah dropped his cards into his lap. "Aw, I was going to bluff, Coach."

"I thought I had a busload of Dolphins," said Coach Reich. "But now I see I'm transporting sharks."

"Groan," said Jonah. "You mean card sharks. I get it."

"What's a card shark?" asked Rosa.

"Never mind," said the coach with a grin. "It's a tired old expression."

Glancing up the aisle toward Mary June, Kristy cleared her throat. "About the roommate change, Coach . . ."

Coach Reich shook his head. "I wish I could help you, Kristy. Neither you nor Rosa is with a parent, and every room has to have a chaperone. I'm afraid the situation is settled."

"Fine," Kristy said, straightening her shoulders. "I'm sure it will work out."

"Thanks for being a good sport," Coach Reich said, turning around. "Mary June has been to a lot of these out-of-town meets. She can show you the ropes."

As Coach Reich moved toward the front of the bus, Mary June inched down the aisle toward the back.

Kristy closed her eyes and pretended to be sleeping.

"I know you're awake," said Mary June.

Kristy opened an eye.

Mary June Williams was perfect. Her blond hair cascaded in rows of shiny curls. Her skin had probably never known a pimple, thought Kristy. And Mary June was a really fast swimmer. The only thing that ruined her perfection was that her favorite hobby was telling the whole world just how perfect she was.

"I beat your record in the freestyle yesterday, Kristy," announced Mary June.

Kristy's other eye flew open.

"You did better than fifty-five seconds?" she demanded.

Mary June blew a perfect pink bubble-gum bubble and nodded.

"Where were you swimming?" asked Kristy.

Mary June shrugged. "In practice. So of course the time didn't count. I didn't mean to make it sound like I'd really beaten you."

Rosa spoke up. "You did make it sound that way, though."

Mary June ignored Rosa and smiled at Kristy. "Sorry."

"That's okay," Kristy said politely. "I get excited when I beat my own time in practice too."

Mary June reached into her pocket. "Want some bubble gum?"

"I don't like bubble gum," Kristy replied. "I like regular chewing gum."

"I'll have to remember that," Mary June said, smiling again. "Since we're going to be roommates."

Kristy reached down into her knapsack and pulled out some candy bars. "Anybody want one of these?"

"I'll take one!" said Rosa.

"Me too," said Jonah.

"You really should save those for quick energy," Mary June advised. In spite of the bus's speed, she stood in the aisle perfectly balanced.

"She's right, Kriss," said Kirk.

"And chocolate is horrible for your complexion," Mary June added. "Of course you don't have to worry about pimples," she said, giving Kristy a look.

Kristy's hand flew up to her nose, where she had a minor eruption. "I don't *usually* have to worry about them," she mumbled.

"Sorry," said Mary June. "I didn't mean to call attention to it."

"That's okay," said Kristy.

"Just thought I'd give you that dietary tip," Mary June said, leaning forward.

"Speaking of tipping," said Jonah, "if you don't get back to your seat, you're going to tip over."

"I'm on my way to the rest room," Mary June said, straightening up. Tossing her hair, she moved toward the back, casting a glance over her shoulder. "I'm really glad we're roommates, Kristy. I've always wanted to get to know you better."

"Gee, she seemed nice," said Rosa once Mary June was out of sight. "Maybe rooming with her won't be so bad."

"I hope not," Kristy said. Sinking into her seat, she held her stomach. "Here comes the motion sickness."

"I'll open the window a little," said Rosa. She reached over and slid the window partway open.

"I hope the driver doesn't mind us wasting the air-conditioning," Kristy said, taking a deep breath. The bus was speeding down a highway next to the beach when she drifted off to sleep.

When Kristy woke up, the bus was turning onto a busy strip. It stopped at a light.

"Are we there yet?" Rosa asked, craning her neck toward the window.

"I'm not sure," said Kristy.

"We're pretty close, I bet," said Kirk.

The strip was lined with hotels, and there was lots of traffic. When the light turned green, the bus moved slowly through the intersection and came to a stop again.

"Looks like we're in a jam," Jonah said.

A piercing squeal filled the air as the public-address system came on. Coach Reich's voice growled over the speaker.

"Now hear this, Dolphins—we're about to disembark at the hotel. I know I don't have to remind you to comport yourselves with dignity. On your way off the bus, please take a schedule. You'll also find the roommate assignments noted there if you don't already know them. Please check in with your chaperone before going anywhere in the hotel. And stay with a buddy.

"After you drop your bags off in your rooms, a light meal is scheduled. Then, at six o'clock this evening, the bus will take us over to the college hosting the event. I think you'll like the pool there."

The microphone squealed again, and the coach's voice was cut off. The bus pulled into the parking lot of a big hotel. Through the window Kristy saw an ocean of other buses filled with kids and their parents.

Kirk whistled. "There's the competition. . . ."

Kristy's heart did a flip. "I can't believe we're here."

Coach Reich's voice broke through again, loud and clear. "Now hear this, Dolphins—welcome to Junior Olympics! I know you'll all make me proud."

"Yay, Coach!" Jonah yelled.

Donna threw her cap in the air.

"Yay, Dolphins!"

Kirk looked over at Kristy. "Congratulations, sis. You made it."

"I haven't done anything yet," said Kristy.

"You had to qualify to compete," her brother reminded her. He looked out the window. "It's an honor just to be here."

# THREE

"Amazing!" said Rosa. "There must be zillions of kids here!"

"That's how it always is at Junior Olympics," said Kirk. "Swimmers come from all over the state."

Edging through the crowd in the hotel lobby, Kristy gazed up at the glass elevators, which were packed with people peering down at them. "Awesome!" she said. "An elevator that you can see out of. I wonder how many floors are in this place."

"It's a pretty tall building," said Jonah. "They've even got palm trees in the lobby."

"And look!" said Rosa. "A fountain!"

"I wonder what the pool here is like," said Kristy.

Coach Reich appeared with Mrs. Williams, Mr. Walsh, and some of the other parents.

"The rooms are ready for us," he said. "We're on the thirtieth floor."

"Let's go," Jonah said, heading for the elevator.

Jonah's dad nabbed him. "Just a minute. The coach isn't finished."

"This is a great hotel," said the coach. "There will be a lot of interesting things for you to check out. There are a number of restaurants off the lobby, including a couple of fast-food places. We'll meet back in the lobby at six o'clock. That should give you enough time to get your gear together and have a light meal. Please keep an eye on your watches. I don't want any stragglers. Tonight is going to be fun."

"All right!" cried Kirk. "Go, Dolphins!"

The team surged toward the bank of glass elevators.

"Please remain with the group," Mrs. Williams called out. Kristy squeezed Rosa's hand and inched forward.

"Hi," said Mary June, coming up behind them. "This is a pretty good hotel. I can show you all around. I've been here before."

Kristy winced. It was bad enough that she was Mary June's roommate. She'd been hoping she wouldn't have to hang out with her.

"The video arcade is somewhere on this floor," Mary June added, bumping up against Kristy. "You and I can check it out together."

"Great," said Kristy, forcing a smile.

Kristy piled into an elevator with Rosa, Mary June, Mrs. Williams, Donna O'Brien, and Donna's mother. As the elevator began to rise, Kristy stared through the glass in amazement.

"What a view!" she exclaimed.

Down below were tons of kids. She could see the tops of their heads. She could see the tops of the palm trees surrounding the fountain. Two other elevators were rising on either side of theirs.

"Look!" Rosa squealed. "There's Jonah and Kirk!"

In the elevator to the right, Kristy could see Kirk and Jonah grinning at them through the glass. Their elevator seemed to be going faster.

"Oh, no," said Kristy with a giggle. "They're going to get there first!"

But the elevators stopped at the same time, and the Dolphins got out on thirty.

"Okay, now I've seen this floor," Jonah said. "Let's go back down to the arcade."

"I want to check out the swimming pool," said Donna.

"Everyone go to your rooms," Coach Reich called over the chatter.

"You girls are in room thirty-two," Mrs. Williams said, handing Mary June a key card. "I'll be in thirty-three. The rooms are adjoining."

"Fine, Mummy," Mary June said.

Mrs. Williams smiled tightly. "Lead the way, Peaches. Of course, I don't have to tell you girls how to behave."

"No, you don't, Mummy," said Mary June.

"I didn't think so," said Mrs. Williams, giving Kristy a bright look.

Kristy followed Mary June and her mother down the corridor. She turned back to wave at Rosa. "See you later."

"Okay," Rosa called back, heading off with Donna and Mrs. O'Brien. "We're in thirty-nine."

"This is it," Mary June said, stopping at a door. She slid the key card into the slot. A little green light went on, and the girls pushed the door open.

"And I'm right next to you," Mrs. Williams reminded them, pushing open her own door. "You girls get unpacked and get your things ready for the meet. I'll check on you in a few minutes."

"You have to excuse my mother," Mary June whispered to Kristy. "She still treats me like I'm a child."

Kristy stood in the doorway and looked into the room. There were two large beds with blue flowered spreads.

"What a pretty room," she remarked.

Mary June tossed one of her bags onto the bed closest

to the television. "Dibs on this one. That is, if it's okay with you?" she said, smiling at Kristy.

"Fine," Kristy said, putting her own things on the bed next to the window.

"Come on," Mary June said, grabbing Kristy by the arm. "I'll show you around the hotel."

"Shouldn't we unpack?" Kristy asked.

"We can do that anytime," Mary June said, tugging her arm.

"What about your mom?" Kristy asked, following Mary June toward the door. "Shouldn't we tell her?"

"Don't bother," said Mary June. "She knows we're together."

The girls stepped into the hallway. The carpets were lush and green.

"Race you down the corridor," said Mary June. She had a mischievous look in her eye. "Outside the concierge lounge on the fifteenth floor, there's a whole room full of vending machines. Everything you could possibly think of."

"Really?" said Kristy.

"Let's hit it!" said Mary June.

She took off running, with Kristy behind her. Kristy decided to go look for Rosa later. The vending machines in the lounge sounded exciting.

The two girls swung around the corner just in time to catch the elevator. They pressed their faces to the glass as it sped down to fifteen.

"This is the place," Mary June announced when the doors opened. "Sugar heaven."

Kristy giggled and followed Mary June to a back hall in which one wall was lined with vending machines. Other kids milled around in front of the machines.

"Rats," said Mary June. "They got here before us. We'd better stock up while we can. There are so many kids at these events, sometimes all the candy gets taken."

Kristy followed her to a huge machine full of candy bars. Mary June opened her purse. Kristy watched in amazement as she dropped quarter after quarter into the machine and candy bars began to fall out.

"Wow!" said Kristy. Her mouth was beginning to water. "You'll never manage to eat all those."

"Sure I will," Mary June said. She counted the candy bars as she stuffed them into her purse.

"How many did you buy?" asked Kristy.

"Fifteen. That should hold me for today. Come on."

"Wait," said Kristy. "I think I'll buy a couple." She fished in her pocket for some change. "I'm not sure how much money I have. I left most of it upstairs."

Mary June offered her a five-dollar bill. "Knock your-self out," she said. "That machine will give you some change."

"Gee, thanks," said Kristy, sliding the bill into the machine.

"Let's get some soda," Mary June said. She un-wrapped a candy bar and took a big bite.

"I thought you told me you only ate chocolate for quick energy," Kristy said. "You said it was bad for the complexion."

"I have the kind of complexion that never breaks out," Mary June said, taking another big bite. "Any-way, I never eat candy at home. And I couldn't eat any on the bus today because my mother was with me. I have to sneak," she confessed. "My mother is militant when it comes to sugar."

"My mom worries about the dentist bills too," said Kristy. "I have to ration my sweets."

"Well, things are even stricter at my house," said Mary June, putting change into the soda machine. "My mother doesn't let me have a speck of sugar."

"Won't she get mad when she sees all this candy you bought?"

"If she finds out about it," said Mary June. "The only reason she let me have gum on the bus today is that I lied and said I had a stomachache."

"Wow," said Kristy. She put a crumpled wrapper in her pocket. "That must be creepy."

Mary June's eyes narrowed. "What's creepy?"

"To have to lie to your mom," said Kristy.

"Lighten up," Mary June said. "You're too serious."

Ripping open the wrapper on her second candy bar, Mary June led Kristy down the corridor. "The entrance to the pool is on this floor too," she said. "Want to see?"

"Sure," said Kristy.

She followed Mary June past a room with washing machines to a door that said CLUB.

"In here," Mary June said, pushing the door open.

The girls walked past a desk piled high with white towels. "May I see your room key?" a young man at the desk asked.

Mary June flashed her key. "No shoes allowed on the pool deck," the man said, looking at the girls' feet.

Mary June kept on walking. "We're not staying," she said. "We just want to look at it."

Noticing the disapproving look on the young man's face, Kristy quickly slipped out of her sneakers.

"Nice pool," she said, trotting behind Mary June.

"Most of the time when I see a pool like this, I want to jump right in," said Mary June. "But on days when I'm having a meet, I like to stay away from the water."

"I feel the same way," said Kristy. "It's as if I want to

save my energy for the race. I don't want to waste it splashing around."

Mary June nodded. "Definitely not. When I get in the water on the day of the meet, it's not for fun. It's serious. Don't you feel that way?"

"Well, kind of," said Kristy.

With a toss of her curls, Mary June turned away. "What event are you swimming tonight?"

"The hundred-yard butterfly," said Kristy.

Mary June chuckled. "You're horrible at the butterfly."

"I know," Kristy said, feeling her cheeks get pink. "I don't expect to do very well. Tomorrow I'll be swimming the freestyle. I'm much better at that."

"The freestyle is my strongest stroke too," Mary June said, walking past the desk with the towels. "I'm probably in the same races that you are tomorrow. Tonight, at least, we can be friends."

"What do you mean?" Kristy asked, scrambling back into her shoes.

"Just a joke," said Mary June. "Just because you compete against someone doesn't mean you have to hate them." She grabbed Kristy by the hand. "I really want us to be friends," she said.

Kristy looked into Mary June's eyes. "Sure," Kristy said with a smile. "We can be friends."

Near the elevators they ran into Kirk and Jonah.

"We found the vending machines," Jonah announced.

"We beat you to it," said Mary June.

Kirk and Jonah ignored Mary June.

"Have you seen the beach out there?" Jonah said. "If only I had my board."

"Maybe the coach will let us have a beach party when we get back to Surfside," Kirk said. "After three days here, we'll probably be ready for a little salt to wash off the chlorine."

"Sounds like fun," said Mary June. "At the party we could all hang out together." Kirk didn't answer. Instead he turned to Kristy.

"Have you got your stuff ready for the meet tonight?" he asked.

Kristy glanced at her watch. "Not yet," she said. "Maybe we'd better go back."

"Fine," said Mary June. She punched the button to bring up an elevator. Two elevators arrived at the same moment.

Jonah jumped into one, dragging Kristy with him. "Let's play elevator tag!"

"Great!" said Kirk, pulling Mary June into the other one. "Mary June's it. Meet you on twenty!"

"What do you mean, I'm it?" Mary June wailed as both doors snapped shut.

"What are we doing?" Kristy asked Jonah. The elevators sped up side by side.

"Elevator tag," he said. "You'll see."

When the door opened on twenty, Kristy and Jonah jumped out. Kirk and Mary June's elevator was just a second behind.

"Run!" Jonah yelled when Mary June stepped out. "She's it!"

Kirk and Jonah took off at a run, and Kristy dashed down the hall after them. Mary June followed them, dropping her candy bars.

"Wait!" she screamed. "I'm dropping all my stuff. This isn't fair!" She chased them around the corner, where another elevator was waiting. Jonah jumped in with Kirk. "So long," Kirk called, waving through the glass. "We'll see you on thirty!"

Mary June got down on her knees and began picking up her candy. "That is the stupidest game," she grumbled.

"I think it's kind of neat," Kristy said, stooping to help her.

"Oh yeah?" Mary June said, giving Kristy's shoulder a punch. "If you think it's so great, you're it."

"Ow," said Kristy, backing off. She stood up and looked at Mary June. "You didn't have to hit me."

"Sorry," Mary June said. "I only meant to tap you."

Kristy rubbed her shoulder. Mary June hadn't hit her hard, but Kristy didn't like getting punched in anger. "It's only a game," Kristy said, walking toward the elevator. "You don't have to take it so seriously."

"You're the serious one," Mary June said, pasting on a smile. She touched Kristy's arm. "Listen, I said I'm sorry. We were playing tag, weren't we?"

Kristy shrugged. "Sure. Forget it. I guess Kirk and Jonah should have asked you before they started the game, anyway."

"Exactly," said Mary June. "It's all their fault. Your brother is really bossy."

"He is bossy sometimes," Kristy admitted. "But I don't think he means anything by it."

When the girls got off on the thirtieth floor, Rosa was waiting outside their room.

"I just knocked on the door, and Mary June's mother is looking for the two of you," she said.

"Oh no," said Kristy.

"Forget it," said Mary June, opening the door with her key. "I'll just make something up."

Kristy turned to Rosa. "Is your room nice?"

"It's great," Rosa replied. "Donna's mom has the

room that's adjoining. She opened the door between the two rooms, so it's just like we've got a suite."

"We have a door between our rooms too. And a really pretty view," Kristy said. "Come on in and see."

Rosa followed Kristy inside. Mary June was dumping her candy bars onto the dresser.

"You can see the ocean!" Rosa exclaimed, looking out the window. She gave Kristy a wistful look. "Want to come over to my room later on and look at the parking lot?"

"Sure," said Kristy.

Mrs. Williams walked into the room. "Just where have you been?" she asked.

"D-Down . . . stairs," stammered Kristy.

"I've been looking for you girls all over the place," said Mrs. Williams. "You have to get your things ready. Then we've got to get something to eat." Her eyes fell on the candy on the dresser.

"What's all this?" she demanded. "There's enough sugar here to sink a boat."

"It's Kristy's," Mary June said, retreating to the armchair.

Kristy's mouth gaped open. The candy bars she had bought were still in her pockets.

Mrs. Williams shook her head at Kristy. "I can't stop you from buying candy," she said, "though I'm sure your mother wouldn't approve. I'll let you keep those candy bars, as long as you don't give any to Mary June."

Kristy stood dumbfounded while Mrs. Williams stroked Mary June's hair. "Be ready for supper soon, Peaches," she said, walking back into her room. "You're going to need your energy tonight."

"Yes, Mummy," Mary June said.

"Don't eat any of Kristy's sweets," Mrs. Williams said, closing the door between the rooms.

"Gee," said Rosa. "She seemed kind of mad."

"Don't pay any attention to her," said Mary June. "She just gets into bad moods."

"Right," muttered Kristy. "How come you didn't tell her these are your candy bars?"

Mary June hung her head. "Sorry. If she found out it was my candy, she'd probably punish me. She can't punish you, because you aren't her daughter. Please don't be mad at me."

Kristy sighed. "Fine, I'll forget it." She walked Rosa to the door.

"Are we still friends?" Mary June called after Kristy.

"Sure," Kristy said, stepping out into the hall.

"How's it going?" Rosa whispered once they were outside the room.

"I don't know," Kristy said quietly. "Mary June says she wants to be friends. But I don't understand her."

"It takes a while to really get to know someone," said Rosa. "Hang in there." She gave Kristy's hand a squeeze.

"Thanks," said Kristy. "Even though you're not my roommate, I'm sure glad you're here."

# FOUR

*Splash!*

Spacing themselves at fifteen-second intervals, the Dolphins took over the warm-up pool at the college. The meet would start in an hour. Skimming along the surface of the water, Kristy felt a pleasant tingling in her arms and legs as her muscles began to wake up. Holding back on her power, she stroked gently, swimming lap after lap. This was only a warm-up. She had to save her energy for later, when she would swim the hundred-yard butterfly stroke.

"How are you feeling?" Rosa asked when Kristy emerged from the pool.

"Great," said Kristy. She pushed her goggles onto her forehead. She was already wearing her turquoise team suit with the orange Dolphins logo.

"Don't forget to hydrate," Rosa said, handing Kristy her water bottle.

"Don't worry," said Kristy, taking a drink. "I'm thirsty."

Kirk came up behind her. "Must have been all that chocolate."

Kristy turned and giggled. "I only ate four candy bars."

Kirk rolled his eyes. "Well, at dinner I hope you ate lots of carbos."

"Don't worry," said Kristy. "Mary June's mother made me eat everything on my plate, including my spinach."

"I'm not surprised," Kirk said. "Mrs. Williams seems kind of strict."

"Maybe too strict," Kristy said. "Mary June is so afraid of her mother getting mad that she lies to her."

"That's too bad," said Kirk. "How about you and Mary June? Are you getting along?"

"Kind of," said Kristy. "She showed me the candy machine."

Kirk laughed. "Be nice to her, Kriss. She doesn't have too many friends. At any rate, not on the Dolphins."

"She doesn't have too many friends at school, either," said Rosa. "She rubs people the wrong way."

"Whatever people think about her, Mary June gives her all when it comes to swimming," Kirk said. "Just try to get along with her if you can."

"Okay," said Kristy. "I'll try."

Coach Reich walked up and patted Kirk on the back. "All ready for tonight?"

"I hope so," said Kirk.

"What event are you swimming?" asked Rosa.

"The two-hundred-yard backstroke," replied Kirk.

"Two hundred yards is a long way!" exclaimed Rosa. "I couldn't imagine backstroking for that distance."

"How are you feeling?" the coach asked, turning to Kristy. "Ready for your first heat in Junior Olympics?"

"I sure feel excited about it," replied Kristy. "Even though the butterfly isn't my strongest stroke."

"It'll be a nice challenge for you," said the coach. "An event like this, with so many races, presents a good opportunity for trying strokes you don't normally compete in."

"That's what my dad said when he helped me sign up for the events a few weeks ago," said Kristy.

"Come on, Rosa," said Coach Reich. "Help me round up the rest of the team. We'll meet at the big pool in ten minutes."

"Yes, sir," Rosa said, skipping away.

"I'm going to check the boys' locker room," said Kirk. "I think Jonah's still in there. You check out the girls' locker room, Kriss."

"Yes, sir," Kristy replied, frowning.

"Sorry," said Kirk. "I don't mean to be bossy."

"That's okay," said Kristy. She touched his arm. "Good luck tonight."

"You too, sis," said Kirk.

Kristy made her way to the girls' locker room. It was filled with swimmers from other teams. She headed toward some turquoise suits in the far corner. Mary June was perched on a stool with her eyes closed while Donna O'Brien talked her through a visualization exercise.

"See yourself walking up to the block," Donna said in a soft voice.

With her eyes still shut, Mary June nodded.

"You look confident. You're well rested and focused."

"I feel great," murmured Mary June.

"Your teammates are smiling at you. They want you to win."

Mary June nodded. "I will."

"Your mother is in the stands. She's smiling at you."

Mary June's eyes flew open. "That's enough," she said, hopping off the stool.

"What's wrong?" asked Donna. "Wasn't the visualization working for you?"

"It was until you put my mother in the picture," said Mary June. She clipped her long hair up into a bun and pulled her cap over it. "I try not to think about my mother being at a meet," she said. "It makes me too nervous."

"Gee," said Kristy. "For me it's just the opposite. Seeing my mom and dad in the crowd makes me feel better. It's when I have to talk to the newspaper reporters that I feel queasy."

"Really?" Mary June said, cocking her head. "It just goes to show how different we are. You need your parents in the crowd and I don't. I love reporters and you're afraid of them."

"I'm not exactly afraid of them," said Kristy. "They just embarrass me."

Mary June shrugged. "Like I said, we're different." She smiled. "I still like you, though."

"Thanks," Kristy said, taking a swig from her water bottle. "We're supposed to meet the coach out at the pool now," she said.

"See you guys later," said Donna, reaching for her gym bag. "I'm going to make a last-minute stop in the bathroom."

Kristy stretched out her arms and legs.

"What are you waiting for?" asked Mary June.

"For you," said Kristy, remembering what Kirk had said about Mary June's needing friends.

Mary June looked surprised. "Thanks," she said, grabbing her towel.

"And good luck tonight," said Kristy.

"Thanks again," said Mary June. "I'm swimming the hundred-yard backstroke. And I have to win tonight."

"Why tonight?" asked Kristy.

Mary June tossed her head. "It's not just tonight," she said. "It's every meet."

Kristy looked at the clock. "We'd better get out there."

Kristy and Mary June walked toward the exit that led to the pool. Mary June reached into her gym bag and gave Kristy a candy bar.

"I've had enough candy," said Kristy.

"Give it to somebody else," said Mary June. "After my mother saw my stash on the dresser, I figured I'd better get rid of the stuff."

Kristy giggled.

"Thanks for not giving me away this afternoon," said Mary June.

The stands surrounding the pool were filled. Each team had staked out a section for swimmers and their parents, and there were lots of other spectators and reporters. Kristy spotted a television camera on one side of the arena.

"Mary June! Mary June! Over here, darling!"

Sitting in the front row of the Dolphins' section, Mrs. Williams flagged them down. She leaped up from her seat and threw her arms around Mary June, barely nodding at Kristy.

"How are you feeling, Peaches?" Mrs. Williams asked, stroking Mary June's arm.

"Leave me alone, Mummy," Mary June muttered. "You're embarrassing me."

"What a silly girl," Mrs. Williams said, touching Mary June's cap. "Are you going to win a gold medal for me?"

Kristy watched Mary June's shoulders grow tense. "Of course I will," Mary June promised.

Slipping away from Mary June and her mother, Kristy found Rosa in the aisle, surrounded by swimmers' blankets, sleeping bags, and gym bags. "They'll be announcing your race soon," Rosa said. "The coach told me to warn you."

Kristy took a deep breath. "Thanks." She looked up at the stands full of people and then at the empty lanes in the pool, where the action would be starting in a few minutes. She closed her eyes and visualized herself walking calmly to the diving block and getting into position for a grab start. She saw herself effortlessly entering the water, her arms stretching out and down. Kristy opened her eyes and rummaged through her gym bag for her heat sheet. She found her name and lane number on it.

"I'm in lane two," she told Rosa, putting the sheet away.

She looked up at the stands and thought about her mother and father. Usually when Kristy swam in a meet, her parents were there. Right before Kristy's race, Dr. Adams would smile and wave her program. As soon as the race was done, she'd make a note of Kristy's time.

"Will you write my time down for me, Rosa?" asked Kristy. "My heat sheet is in my bag. After the race I might be so excited that I forget to."

"Sure," said Rosa.

"Ready?" Coach Reich asked, walking up to Kristy.

Kristy adjusted her goggles. "Ready." She looked back one last time at the team. Kirk was sitting on his sleeping bag, playing cards with Jonah. Kirk looked up and gave Kristy the high sign. Kristy waved back and walked to the deck of the pool.

As she got closer to the starting block, her stomach knotted just for an instant. In her first race, Kristy had gotten so nervous that she had lost her concentration and swum into the wall. But tonight she felt just the right amount of excitement to give her an edge. As the other girls in the race began to take their places, Kristy walked toward lane two. Stepping up, she got into position, curling her toes over the front edge of the starting block. She grabbed the front of the block on either side of her feet. She took a breath and waited for the signal.

A voice sounded over the speakers: "Swimmers, take your marks." Seconds later, the starting beeper went off. Using all the strength in her legs for momentum, Kristy reached out. Gliding through the air, she sliced into the water and began to kick, breathing only after her first arm stroke. A hundred-yard swim was back and forth across the pool twice.

Kirk was standing on the sidelines, keeping his eye on his sister and on the clock. Though the race was timed in seconds, for the spectators it could seem like an eternity.

"She's coming in," Kirk said, leaning forward.

"Lane five is catching up, though!" exclaimed Jonah.

"Come on, Kristy," breathed Rosa. "Come on!"

Kristy couldn't hear them. She was in her own world in lane two. The only things on her mind were her stroke, her kick, and the water.

She touched the wall for the final time. Kirk and Rosa jumped up. Kristy had come in fourth.

"Yay, Kristy!" shouted Rosa.

"Look at that time!" cried Kirk. "One-ten-fifty-nine! Just under one minute and eleven seconds! That's phenomenal!"

"And the butterfly isn't even Kristy's best stroke!" said Rosa.

Kristy climbed out of the pool and walked over to Coach Reich. He handed her a towel.

"You were wonderful, Kriss," said the coach. "Your turns were fast, and you had a great start."

"Thanks," said Kristy, smiling. She blinked as the official timer at the end of her lane gave her a card with her time.

"Wow! I can't believe it," said Kristy, looking at the numbers on the card and then at the board. "I—I can't believe it," she stammered, looking at the coach. "I didn't think I was any good at the fly."

"You were tonight," said Coach Reich. "Your first event at Junior Olympics. A few seconds faster and you might have won a bronze."

Kristy joined the rest of the team. "Nice going, sis!" said Kirk.

"Give me five!" said Jonah, slapping her hand.

Rosa waved Kristy's heat sheet in the air. "I wrote down the time."

"I wish Mom and Dad were here," said Kirk. "They'd be proud of you."

"Thanks, Kirk," Kristy said, swallowing a lump in her throat. It would have been nice to have her parents see her make such a good time.

A voice on the loudspeaker announced the start of the next event. Kristy went to get her sweatshirt. Mary June was stretching her legs in a corner.

"When are you up?" Kristy asked.

"Soon," Mary June muttered. She looked at Kristy with narrowed eyes. "That race you swam was pure luck. That happens once in a while."

Kristy swallowed. "I guess I was lucky. Hope my luck holds until tomorrow."

"Don't count on it," said Mary June. "It's when you really think you're going to win that you don't."

"Really?" said Kristy.

"Sorry," said Mary June, standing up. "I don't mean to jinx you. You did a good job just now." She shivered and hugged her arms.

"Are you cold?" Kristy asked, offering her a towel.

"I always get cold when I'm nervous," Mary June admitted. She looked out at the pool and frowned. "Sometimes I get so nervous, I feel like I'm going to throw up."

"To tell the truth," said Kristy, "so do I." She giggled. "Thank goodness it hasn't happened yet."

Mrs. Williams came over to the girls. "Leave Mary June alone, Kristy," she said. "She has to keep her focus."

"Sure, Mrs. Williams," said Kristy, moving down the aisle to sit next to Donna.

"Poor Mary June," Kristy whispered. "She's really nervous."

"I think her mother makes things worse," said Donna. She offered Kristy a bagel. "Mrs. Walsh gave this to me. Want it? I'm pretty sure it'll get stuck in my braces."

"Gee, thanks. I love bagels, and we never get them at home," said Kristy, taking the bagel. "Is your event coming up soon?"

"I've got a wait," Donna said, looking down at her heat sheet. She pointed toward the pool. "Look, they're about to start the women's hundred-yard backstroke."

"Mary June is in one of those heats," Kristy said, leaning forward.

Sure enough, Mary June was on deck down by the pool. Kristy watched her adjusting her goggles. Her mouth was drawn tight as if she was angry.

"Mary June has the killer instinct," Donna said.

"She's a good swimmer," said Kristy.

"I guess the officials think so too," said Donna. "They've put her in lane five."

Kristy watched Mary June walk up to the center lane, reserved for the fastest swimmers. Mary June slipped into the water and grasped the backstroke bar, hanging motionless with her feet on the wall.

Again a voice crackled over the loudspeaker: "Swimmers, take your positions." Mary June pulled her body and head closer to her hands. The beeper sounded for the start and she pushed away, her body stretching above the water before entering it smoothly.

The formation of swimmers took the shape of a V as the stronger swimmers in the middle lanes broke out and raced for the opposite wall.

"She's in the lead already," said Donna.

"She's going all out," said Kristy. "I think she might place."

"Here comes lane six," said Donna, standing up.

"Lane three is coming in second," said Kristy. "Hey, look—Mary June is next!"

"Come on, Mary June!" Kristy heard Kirk cheer. "Come on, Dolphins!"

"She did it!" Kristy said, giving Donna a hug. "She came in third!"

Cheers erupted from the Dolphins' section. Mary June looked very serious when she got out of the water and talked to the timer. Kristy watched while Coach Reich walked over to her.

"I'm going to go congratulate her," Kristy said.

"Did you see that?" Kirk said, catching Kristy's arm as she walked past. "The Dolphins are going to rack up some points."

"Now it's up to you and Jonah to put us over the top," Kristy teased, giving Kirk a thumbs-up.

Kristy waited for Mary June to come up from poolside. Mrs. Williams was standing close by, holding two towels.

"Better luck next time, sweetie," Mrs. Williams said, going to meet Mary June. "If only you hadn't slowed up at the end. I was sure you were going to come in first or even second."

Tears sprang to Mary June's eyes. Kristy suddenly felt sorry for her.

"Congratulations," Kristy said, reaching out to her.

Mary June shrugged and kept on walking. "Thanks," she said, "but I guess I should have done better."

# FIVE

Back at the hotel, the Dolphins huddled in the corner of the lobby and kept their eyes on Coach Reich.

"This is a gold-letter night for our team," the coach said, rubbing his chin. "You guys must have had some cod liver oil for supper and sprouted fins."

The team laughed. "Cod liver oil—yuk!" Donna called out. "How about some pasta?"

"Sure thing," said the coach. "If you noodleheads haven't put the pasta place out of business."

"What's a noodlehead?" Rosa whispered.

"A kind of dolphin," Kirk replied seriously. "I read about them in *National Geographic*."

Jonah howled, and the whole team laughed. Rosa blushed.

"Well, dolphins or noodleheads," the coach said with a grin, "I'm very proud of all of you. Before you get your late snack, I think our winners for this evening deserve some recognition. Come on up," he called with a wave. "Kirk Adams racked up a lot of points for the team with his silver medal tonight in the two-hundred-yard backstroke. In the same event, Jonah Walsh received a bronze. Mary June Williams got a bronze in the hundred-yard backstroke."

Mary June scooted to the front, followed by Jonah and Kirk. The three of them displayed their medallions, which hung on red, white, and blue ribbons. Kristy and the rest of the team applauded.

"Everyone on the Dolphins was a winner tonight," the coach continued. "You did your best. I'd especially like to mention Kristy Adams's outstanding time in the hundred-yard fly and greased-lightning Donna O'Brien in the two-hundred-yard free. Though these girls didn't receive medals, they beat their own best times by remarkable margins. And everyone on the team displayed good sportsmanship. In my book, good sportsmanship gets a lot of points."

Jonah raised his hand. "Hey, Coach . . . can we go now? My stomach's kind of growling."

"I get the hint," said Coach Reich. "I'll let you guys go. After you eat, get straight to bed. We've got to leave for the pool tomorrow morning at five-thirty A.M. Good night."

Turning on his heel, Coach Reich waved good-bye, and the team broke up into groups.

"Which restaurant is your group going to?" Kristy asked Rosa.

"The pasta place," Rosa replied. "Right, Donna?"

"My mom said she was going to take us there," Donna answered. "I hope they have fettuccine."

"We'll go there too," Jonah said, smiling at Rosa. "Okay, Kirk?"

"I'm up for it," said Kirk. He looked at Kristy. "Coming with us, sis?"

"Do you want to go with them?" Kristy asked Mary June.

Mary June shrugged. "Sure. Why not?"

"You might want to make a stop in the room first," Mrs. Williams suggested. "Both you girls have damp hair."

Kristy felt her ponytail. "I don't have to," she said. "My hair's almost dry."

"So is mine, Mummy," Mary June said, smoothing her curls back. "Let's just go. Please."

"Fine," said Mrs. Williams. "But as soon as you eat, we go upstairs."

The pasta restaurant was crowded with Dolphins as well as swimmers from other teams. Kirk, Jonah, Rosa, and Kristy ran ahead to grab a booth. Donna and her mother took a small table behind them. Mrs. Williams and Mr. Walsh sat at a table across the aisle. "What about me?" Mary June said, ambling up to the booth. She tapped her foot. "Where am I going to sit?"

"Sit here," Kristy said, squeezing in closer to Rosa. "There's always room for one more."

"I wonder if they sell french fries here," said Rosa.

"Sure they do," said Kirk. "Didn't you know that potato is a form of pasta?"

Rosa raised her eyebrows. "It is?"

"Of course," Jonah said. "Not only that, but potatoes are the favorite food of the noodlehead dolphin."

"You've got to be kidding," said Rosa.

"Oh, brother," Mary June said with a snicker. "You're so gullible."

When the waitress appeared, Kristy ordered fettuccine Alfredo and a large Coke.

"Are you sure you should order Coke this late?" Kirk said.

"I'll be fine," said Kristy. "Nothing could keep me from sleeping tonight."

The others ordered pasta too. As soon as the waitress left, Jonah made a paper airplane out of his place mat and sent it sailing toward Donna. A second later the airplane sailed back. Across the aisle, Mrs. Williams wagged her finger.

"Better stop," Mary June whispered. "Or my mom will come over."

"Your mother is strict," said Rosa.

"She's only trying to be a good chaperone," Mary June said, bristling.

The pasta came, and everyone dug in.

"You eat as if you're starving to death, Rosa," Kirk said. How come you're so hungry? You didn't even swim."

"I'm not sure," Rosa said, chewing. "You guys put out so much energy, I think it takes energy just watching you."

"All right," Jonah said, pushing his plate away. "On to the video arcade."

"Great!" said Kristy, scraping the last ounce of sauce off her plate.

"I love the video arcade in this hotel," Mary June said. "I've stayed here before."

"Yes, we know," said Rosa. "You've told us."

They all stood up and moved out of the booth. "We're going to the arcade," Mary June called out to her mother and Mr. Walsh.

"I'll go with you," said Mr. Walsh. "But you can only stay for twenty minutes."

"Twenty minutes!" Jonah exclaimed. "Oh, Dad . . ."

"We'll go too," said Mrs. O'Brien.

"Okay, Mummy?" Mary June said. Running to her

mother's side, she stuck out her hand. "I think Kristy and I might need some extra money."

Mrs. Williams shook her head. "Sorry, but I don't think you and Kristy can go."

"We can't?" Kristy blurted out. "Oh, please, Mrs. Williams."

"I'm sorry," Mary June's mother said, patting her lips with a napkin. "Mary June needs plenty of rest the night before a meet. And I'm sure you do too." She patted Mary June's hand. "You understand, don't you, Peaches?"

Mary June nodded glumly.

Crossing to the booth where the girls had been sitting, Mrs. Williams picked up the checks for Kristy's and Mary June's meals.

"See you guys in the morning," Kristy said, waving to Rosa, Donna, Jonah, and Kirk.

"Sorry you can't go, sis," Kirk said as he hurried out. "But maybe it's just as well. You have trouble waking up, and we've got to get out of here at the crack of dawn."

Mrs. Williams paid the cashier, and Kristy and Mary June followed her out of the restaurant. The lobby was swarming with swimmers just back from the meet.

"Maybe we can play cards," Kristy suggested. They

got into the elevator, and Mrs. Williams pressed the button for thirty.

"I have another idea," Mary June whispered into Kristy's ear.

Mrs. Williams followed the girls into their room. "I'm going to take a shower, girls," she announced, opening the door between the two rooms. "You two get ready for bed."

"All right, Mummy," Mary June said. "We're going to sleep as fast as we can."

"We are?" Kristy groaned, throwing herself onto her bed.

"Of course we are," Mary June said so that her mother would hear. She closed the door between the two rooms.

"Want to go to the arcade?" Mary June asked, rushing over to Kristy.

Kristy sighed. "Maybe tomorrow after the meet there will be a chance."

"There's plenty of time left tonight," Mary June said, looking at her watch.

"Your mom said we couldn't go," said Kristy.

"Stuff your pillows under the sheets," Mary June instructed, rumpling her own bed.

Kristy stared as Mary June arranged her pillows under the covers. "Why are you doing that?"

Mary June stood back from her handiwork. "Use your imagination. What does it look like?" she said.

Kristy shook her head and giggled. With the pillows and bunched-up covers, Mary June had made it look as if a person were in the bed.

"All we have to do is turn out the light," Mary June whispered. "When my mom comes in to check on us, she'll see the pillows under the covers and think we're sleeping."

"Wow," Kristy said, "that's pretty cool. But . . . won't we get in trouble when she finds out it's not us in the bed?"

"Relax," Mary June said. She quickly arranged Kristy's bed so that it looked like her own. "We're only going to be gone for a little while. By the time we get back, she'll probably still be in the shower."

Kristy bit her lip. "I do want to stop by the video arcade."

"Everybody else is doing it," Mary June said. "Why shouldn't we? The worst that can happen is that my mom will get mad at me."

"At us, you mean," said Kristy.

"Come on," said Mary June, turning off the lights. "If we get caught, I'll tell her it's my fault."

Quietly opening the door, the two girls slipped out of the room.

"Let's go!" Mary June said, running down the hall. "The arcade is on the ground floor!"

"Wait," Kristy said, stopping suddenly. "I forgot my key."

"Don't worry," Mary June said, punching the elevator button. "I have mine."

Stepping into the glass elevator, Kristy felt a wave of giddiness. It was hard to believe that she'd left home only that afternoon. A lot had happened. She'd gotten a really good time in a stroke she normally didn't compete in, and she was getting to be friends with Mary June, which was also surprising. And the day wasn't over.

It didn't take the girls long to find Kirk, Jonah, Rosa, and Donna clustered around one of the games. Mr. Walsh and Mrs. O'Brien were at the refreshment stand buying bottles of spring water.

"Hey, Kriss!" Kirk called. "Come and see this! A game called The Human Shark!"

"The Human Shark!" Kristy repeated, running over. "That sounds awesome."

"How do you play it?" Mary June asked, crowding in.

"I'll show you in a minute," Kirk promised, "as soon as Jonah stops hogging the game."

"You already played," Jonah argued. "I even paid for

your game. Now, give me some arm room," he added, pushing the controls. "I'm trying to get to a new level."

Ducking in front of Kirk, Kristy fixed her eyes on the screen. Two swimmers were racing side by side in an ocean full of small fish. One of the swimmers had a net. The object was to have the swimmer with the net catch as many fish as she could and still win the race. Kristy leaned in closer as Jonah worked the controls. The swimmer with the net was falling back.

"Oh, no!" Jonah cried as the other swimmer gained. "I'm going to get it!"

The game began to honk and ring. Kristy's eyes widened as one of the swimmers turned into a shark and ate the one with the net.

"Darn it!" Jonah said as the game clicked off. "I'm still just at level four."

"That's the weirdest game I ever saw," said Mary June.

"It's gruesome," said Rosa.

"I want to play it," said Kristy.

"After me," said Kirk. "It's my turn."

Mr. Walsh and Mrs. O'Brien came over with the spring water. A man with a camera was with them.

"Here they are," Mr. Walsh announced, putting an arm around Jonah. "This is Charles Flowers. He's a reporter for *The Surfside Gazette.* And these are the Dolphins."

"How do you do?" Kirk said, stepping forward. "I think I remember you. You're the one who thought up the name the Nuclear Adams."

Kirk and Kristy exchanged a quick grin. Because their father was a college professor, when he'd first seen the phrase "the Nuclear Adams" in the weekly *Surfside Gazette*, he'd pointed out that it wasn't grammatical. "Actually, since there are two of you, you'd be the Nuclear *Adamses,*" he'd said. Kirk and Kristy had rolled their eyes—their father was always correcting their grammar too.

"You have a good memory," said the reporter, flashing a smile at Kirk. "Mind if I get a group shot?"

"Not at all," said Mary June, stepping forward. She extended her hand. "I'm Mary June Williams. *Mary June* is two words."

"I saw you tonight," said the reporter. "Nice going. If you'll just squeeze in with the others."

Mary June stood in front of the group, while Kristy half hid behind Kirk.

"Everybody say 'Fish,' " said the reporter.

They all said "Fish" and broke up laughing.

"Thanks a lot," the reporter said. "Now, just a quick one of the Nuclear Adams."

"Fine," Kirk said, grabbing Kristy's hand. The rest of the group cleared away. Kristy felt her face getting red.

"Got it!" the reporter said, clicking his camera again. "Thanks, everybody. Good job today. I'll be at the meet tomorrow." He pointed to Kristy. "You surprised us today in that butterfly event. I love watching you."

"Thanks," muttered Kristy.

"I really don't know what the deal is with that reporter," Mary June said. "He only seems to pay attention to Kirk and Kristy, just because they're brother and sister."

"That's not entirely true," said Mr. Walsh. "He gives the whole team quite a bit of coverage."

"We might as well face it," Mrs. O'Brien said, giving Kristy a pat on the shoulder. "The Nuclear Adams are stars."

Mr. Walsh waved his arm at Jonah and Kirk. "Time for bed."

"Haven't you heard?" said Jonah. "Dolphins don't sleep."

"These Dolphins do," Mr. Walsh said, laughing and grabbing the two boys by the arm.

"Bedtime for us, too," said Mrs. O'Brien, leaving with Rosa and Donna in tow. She glanced back at Mary June. "Does your mother know you're still down here?"

"Don't worry," said Mary June. "We're going right up."

"I wish we didn't have to go up," Kristy said once the others had gone. She stared at The Human Shark. "I really wanted to try this game. It's hysterical."

"Go ahead," said Mary June. "A few more minutes won't hurt."

"Are you sure it's all right?" asked Kristy.

Mary June smiled. "Sure. I bet you can't get to level six."

Kristy put some quarters into the slot. She grabbed the controls and watched the two swimmers take off. "This is so stupid!" she howled, trying to catch fish with the net. The second swimmer passed her right away.

"Oh, no, here it comes!" she said.

"Hurry up!" Mary June said. "Hurry up!"

The second swimmer turned into a shark, leaping lane after lane. The machine honked and beeped, and the first swimmer got eaten.

"Level two," Kristy moaned. "How did Jonah get to level four? I want to try it again."

"You can," Mary June said slyly. "I'll just go up and check that everything is okay with my mother. Then I'll come back down for you."

"Really?" said Kristy. "Thanks."

"Don't mention it," Mary June said, hurrying away.

Kristy got more change from the machine and went back to the game. It took her three more tries to get to level three.

"I'm getting better," she muttered, going back to the change machine. Suddenly she realized how quiet it was. There were very few kids left in the arcade.

*Mary June said she would come and get me,* Kristy thought as she poured quarter after quarter into the video machine. *I'll just play until I get to level five.*

Instead, Kristy played until she ran out of money.

"Well, at least I got to level six," she said to herself with a yawn. She glanced down at her watch. "One-thirty!" she gasped. What had happened to Mary June?

Running out into the lobby, Kristy took the elevator to the thirtieth floor. Not until she was in front of her door did she remember that she had no key. Her heart beating fast, she knocked softly.

"Mary June!" she whispered. "Mary June! It's me! Open up!"

The door clicked open. Mrs. Williams was standing there in her nightgown.

"Kristy, what on earth are you doing out in the hall?" she said crossly, rubbing her eyes. "You're supposed to be in bed. Don't wake Mary June."

"Sorry," Kristy said. "I won't." She crept into the room.

"Change in the bathroom," whispered Mrs. Williams. She scowled at Kristy again and then disappeared into her room.

Opening the dresser drawer as quietly as she could, Kristy felt around for her pajamas. Then, slipping into the bathroom, she clicked on the light and got changed. She glanced at herself in the mirror with a guilty expression. She knew that what she had done was wrong. If the coach found out, he would be angry. He might even pull her from Junior Olympics!

Slipping back into the bedroom, she pulled the pillows from under her covers. In the other bed, Mary June was sound asleep.

## SIX

"Kristy, wake up! Kristy!"

Kristy groaned and buried herself in the covers. "No, Mom, not now. It's too early."

"You're not at home," Kristy heard a voice say. "You're in a hotel. It's me, Mrs. Williams."

Kristy's eyes flew open. She shot up like a bolt. "What time is it?" she asked. "Did I miss the meet?"

Sitting on her bed, Mary June swung her legs lazily. "You will miss the meet, if you don't get up."

"You've got ten minutes to dress," said Mrs. Williams.

Struggling to disentangle her legs from the sheets, Kristy gazed bleary-eyed at Mary June and her mother. They were both dressed, and Mary June's bed was made.

Kristy's feet hit the floor. She looked around for her suit. It wasn't on the air conditioner, where she'd left it.

"Your suit is in your bag," Mrs. Williams said. "Pull on some clothes and brush your teeth. Peaches and I will give you some privacy."

Mary June and her mother went into Mrs. Williams's

room. Relieved to be left alone, Kristy rummaged through her drawer and pulled out a T-shirt, shorts, and underwear. Stumbling into the bathroom, she splashed her face with water to wake herself up. In the mirror she saw dark circles under her eyes.

"What a noodlehead I am," she muttered. The coach had told them to get a good rest, but thanks to The Human Shark, Kristy had slept less than four hours.

"Hurry up!" Mary June's voice came through the door. "We have to go eat."

"I'm coming," Kristy said, pulling on her T-shirt.

When she got out of the bathroom, Mary June and her mother were standing at the door.

"Don't forget this," Mrs. Williams said, giving Kristy her bag. "Your team suit and caps are inside. So are your goggles."

"Thanks," said Kristy.

"You're welcome," said Mrs. Williams. She eyed Kristy sternly. "I'm sure your mother would do the same for Mary June. Though I don't imagine Mary June would have stayed up until after one A.M. the night before a meet."

"Sorry," Kristy muttered. "It was dumb."

Down in the hotel's coffee shop, Kristy was glad to see the other Dolphins, especially Kirk. He was sitting at the counter with empty seats on either side of him.

"Hi, Kirk," she said, running over. "Can I sit here?"

"Jonah and Rosa asked me to save these seats for them," Kirk said. "Why don't you sit with Mary June?"

"I don't want to," Kristy said, feeling a catch in her throat. "I want to sit with you. Jonah can sit with his mom. Please."

Kirk looked at Kristy closely. "Sure. Everything okay? You really shouldn't be worried about your race this morning. You were in excellent shape last night."

"This morning I'm kind of tired," Kristy admitted.

"You never were a morning person," Kirk teased. "What do you want for breakfast?"

"Orange juice, a muffin, and a bagel," said Kristy. "I'll buy some snacks when we get to the pool."

Kirk put in their order. Kristy glanced over at Mrs. Williams. She was buttering a muffin for Mary June. If Mrs. Williams told Coach Reich about Kristy's staying up so late, Kristy would be in big trouble. Kristy looked over at Kirk.

"Eat your muffin," he said. "We've got to meet the coach any minute."

Kristy forced herself to take a bite. "I'm not too hungry. I didn't sleep much last night."

"Too excited?" Kirk asked, gulping his orange juice.

"Not exactly," said Kristy. She wanted to tell him what she'd done but decided against it. Kirk did everything according to the rules. If he found out she'd sneaked out of her room and stayed up half the night, he'd be mad.

"Then how come you didn't sleep?" Kirk asked her.

"I had bad dreams," Kristy said.

Kirk patted her shoulder. "Too bad."

"That's okay," Kristy said, smiling weakly. "Anyway, I got to level six on The Human Shark."

"No kidding," said Kirk. "That's a fun game. We'll have to play it again."

"Time to get going, Kristy," Mrs. Williams called.

"I'll go with Kirk," Kristy called back.

Mrs. Williams nodded.

At exactly five-thirty, the Dolphins met Coach Reich at the bus and headed for the pool.

"What event are you swimming this morning?" Rosa asked, taking a seat next to Kristy.

"The fifty-yard freestyle," Kristy answered. She looked into her best friend's dark eyes. "Oh, Rosa . . ."

"What is it?" asked Rosa.

"I think I'm sick," said Kristy.

Rosa felt her forehead. "You don't have a fever."

"I have a stomachache," said Kristy.

"From motion sickness?" asked Rosa.

"Not exactly," said Kristy. She yawned. "I wish I'd been your roommate, though. I think I'm in lots of trouble."

"For what?" asked Rosa.

"For staying up when I shouldn't have," said Kristy. "I'm sure Mrs. Williams will tell the coach."

Rosa reached into her knapsack and got out some chewing gum. "Chew this. It will make you feel better."

"But what if I get in trouble?" said Kristy. "What will I do?"

"Say you're sorry," said Rosa. "Maybe you should try not to think about it. You should keep your mind on your race."

"You're right," said Kristy. "I'm not in trouble yet. It might not even happen. I should concentrate on my swimming."

"Need some more gum?" asked Rosa.

Kristy yawned and closed her eyes. "What I really need is some sleep."

Five minutes later, Rosa was nudging her arm.

"We're here already?" Kristy said, rubbing her eyes. "Why does the meet have to start so early?"

"Don't worry," Rosa said as they moved into the

aisle. "Once you get into the warm-up pool, you'll wake up."

When Kristy got off the bus, Mary June was waiting next to Coach Reich.

"How are you feeling this morning, Kristy?" asked the coach.

Kristy swallowed a yawn. "Great."

"I just wanted you to know that you and Mary June are part of the freestyle relay team tomorrow."

"Really?" said Kristy. "Thanks!"

"Who's the anchor?" Mary June asked.

"Kristy will be the anchor," the coach replied.

"Wow!" Kristy exclaimed. "Thanks a lot, Coach."

"Yeah, thanks a lot," Mary June muttered.

"You girls are both working very hard," said Coach Reich. "I know I can depend on you. But the relay is not until tomorrow. Let's think about today. I want to see some fast times in the preliminaries this morning. Though I don't think either of you will have trouble qualifying for this afternoon's finals."

"I got a great night's sleep," said Mary June. "You can certainly count on me." Kristy gave her a sideways look but didn't say anything.

After checking in at the table in the lobby, the girls headed for the locker room. Kristy felt alert and excited. The coach's news that she would be swimming anchor for the relay the following day had sent adrenaline pumping through her system. But she was still worried about what had happened the night before.

"Do you think your mother is going to tell Coach Reich about last night?" Kristy asked Mary June.

"I asked her not to," said Mary June.

"Gee, thanks," Kristy said with a sigh of relief. "I was never so shocked in my life as when she opened the door."

"Sorry about that," said Mary June. "I guess I was sleeping."

The girls got into their suits.

"I completely lost track of time playing that video game," Kristy confessed. "You said you were going to come back for me. What happened?"

Mary June looked away. "My mom was walking into the room when I came back. I had to jump into bed really quickly."

"Did she find out about how we stuffed the beds with pillows?" Kristy asked.

"I'm not sure," said Mary June. "Anyway, she doesn't think I did it."

Kristy swallowed. "I guess there's no sense in our both getting into trouble."

"Precisely," said Mary June. "Besides, Mummy has said she won't say a thing about you. She said that if you were too tired to swim a good race, it would be a good lesson for you."

"But I *am* going to swim a good race," Kristy said, forcing a smile. "I feel just great."

Leaving Mary June behind, Kristy dashed off to the warm-up pool. She stretched out her legs and did sit-ups. Then she slipped into the pool. The water was cold. Kristy sprinted a couple of laps.

"You're going to tire yourself out," Rosa warned as Kristy touched the wall.

"I've got to get my body moving," Kristy explained. "It feels like lead."

Kristy slowed down her strokes, but her heart was still beating fast. The race she would swim that morning required lots of energy. After her sleepless night, she hoped that when the time came, she would have it.

After her warm-up Kristy put on some sweats and went out to rest in the Dolphins' section. Rosa was helping the coach check in a late swimmer, and Kirk was still in the pool. Curling up in her seat, Kristy covered her knees with her sleeping bag. The sounds in the crowded stadium grew distant as she dozed off.

She felt a hand on her shoulder. "Your event is coming up soon." It was Coach Reich. He was wearing a gentle smile. "Better get up and walk around for a few minutes."

"Right," said Kristy. She jumped up and took a swig from her water bottle.

Rosa walked over to her, unwrapping a Power Bar.

"Need some energy?" she asked.

Kristy nodded and broke off a piece. The bar was sweet, but it didn't make her any less tired.

A voice came over the loudspeaker, announcing Kristy's event: "Eleven- and twelve-year-old women's fifty-yard freestyle."

Kristy pulled off her sweatshirt and yanked her goggles over her eyes.

"Good luck," said Rosa.

Kristy smiled.

The tiles were cold on the bottoms of her feet, but perspiration popped out on her forehead. As she walked toward the starting block, her knees felt weak. She tried to picture herself making a good, clean start with her teammates watching and smiling. But her mind flooded instead with images from The Human Shark, along with a picture of Mrs. Williams's scowling face.

Taking her place in lane five, she got into position.

The voice on the loudspeaker said, "Take your mark!" *Beep!* Her body jolted into a dive.

The first length didn't seem hard. Her body hummed as she started the second. But halfway through, Kristy's energy vanished. Every stroke and kick was a huge effort. Realizing that she was falling behind, she panicked and pushed herself to catch up. Her arms felt weak as she pulled herself out of the pool at the end of the lap. Several swimmers had come in before her. The timer at the end of her lane handed Kristy her card and gave her her time: 29.90 seconds.

"Thanks," said Kristy. As she walked toward Coach Reich, she kept her chin up and tried not to show how disappointed she was in her time.

"You fought hard," Coach Reich said, putting her sweatshirt around her shoulders. "But you died out there. Always remember to keep something in reserve for that last sprint."

"I know, Coach," said Kristy. "I'll do better next time."

When she came off the deck, Kirk met her. "Good work," he said. "You tried."

"I've had faster times than that," Kristy said, batting back her tears. "I won't be able to swim tonight. Only the eight fastest swimmers qualify."

"You might," said Kirk, looking out at the pool. "Let's watch the next heat."

Mary June was lining up for the next race. It was part of the same event Kristy had swum in. Kristy and Kirk fixed their eyes on the swimmers as the starting beeper sounded.

"Mary June looks wonderful," said Kristy. "She seems to skim over the water."

"She's a great swimmer," said Kirk. He put an arm around Kristy's shoulder. "But so are you. You were just a little off this morning."

Kristy's body tensed as she watched the eight swimmers in the pool swim the same race she'd just finished. As they came in one by one, she and Kirk watched the board for their times. Mary June came in second in her group with a time of 27.49 seconds.

"Wow," said Kristy. "She did great!"

Kirk took Kristy's card and checked it against the times on the board.

"How did I do?" asked Kristy.

"You just made it. You're still in the running," said Kirk.

Kristy looked at the times on the board. "You're right," she said. She had come in eighth. "I could have done better. But I could have done worse," she said, sighing. "I guess I can't expect much with just four hours of sleep."

"Four hours of sleep?" said Kirk.

"I was playing The Human Shark," Kristy said, hanging her head. "It's my own fault that I got such a poor time."

"It sure is," Kirk snapped. "Lots of kids would have

loved to swim at Junior Olympics. I can't believe you'd disobey the coach's training instructions to play a dumb video game."

"I couldn't stop playing it," Kristy argued. "And Mary June said—"

"Don't try to blame Mary June," said Kirk. "Just concentrate on doing your best for the rest of the meet. It took a lot of hard work for us to become the Nuclear Adams."

He stalked off and left her standing there.

"I need a buddy to go with me to the concession stand," Rosa said, appearing at her side. "They've got some awesome T-shirts."

"I'll go with you," Kristy said glumly.

Outside in the lobby, Rosa bought a key chain in the shape of a seashell. "That's for Mom," she told Kristy.

"Cute," said Kristy. "I wish I could get one for my mother. But I can't, because I spent all my money. I spent a bundle on The Human Shark last night." She blushed. "Mary June's mother didn't give us permission. I shouldn't even have been down there."

"Is that why you thought you were going to get in trouble?" asked Rosa.

"Yes," said Kristy.

With his camera case on his shoulder, Charles Flowers appeared out of the crowd.

"Tough luck this morning," he said to Kristy.

"Thanks," Kristy said in a low voice.

"What happened?" the reporter asked. "Yesterday evening you seemed charmed."

"I stayed up too late," Kristy blurted out. "I was playing video games."

The reporter grinned. "I guess that's an occupational hazard when you come to these meets. Do you like video games?"

"Unfortunately, I love them," said Kristy.

"Well, good luck tonight," the reporter said. As he walked away, he jotted something down.

"Oh, no," said Kristy. "Now what have I done?"

"What's wrong?" asked Rosa.

"I told that reporter I was downstairs playing video games last night. What if he writes about it in the paper? The coach will read it. It'll come out that I stayed out until after one. Mom and Dad might even read about it."

"Calm down," said Rosa. "Try not to think about the newspapers."

"You're right," said Kristy. "This afternoon all I'm going to think about is taking a nap. I just hope I swim better tonight."

"Look on the bright side," said Rosa. "You can't swim worse."

# SEVEN

"What a great morning!" Mary June said, bouncing onto her bed when the girls got back to their room. "I love it when I swim well."

"You were good, all right," Kristy said, sinking into the armchair. "I only wish I hadn't punked out in my heat."

Mary June shrugged. "You did your best."

"That's the thing. The time I got wasn't close to my best," Kristy said, rolling her eyes. "I've got to take a nap this afternoon or I'll be too tired to put on my goggles tonight."

Mary June giggled and tweaked Kristy's hair. "You are so funny sometimes. Just because you did a horrible job this morning doesn't mean that your energy won't come back."

Kristy winced.

"Sorry," said Mary June. "I didn't mean to rub it in."

"It's okay," said Kristy, pulling off her shoes. "It's my own fault that I stayed up playing video games."

"Speaking of which—" Mary June looked at herself

in the mirror and bared her teeth. "How about a game of The Human Shark?" she growled.

Kristy laughed halfheartedly. "Maybe tomorrow after the meet is all over. Right now I've got to get some sleep."

Kristy pulled down the covers. "Don't tell me you're actually going to get in bed?" said Mary June.

"I'm not going to sleep on the floor, if that's what you mean," said Kristy, stretching out on the bed. When her head sank into the pillow, she sighed.

"I can't believe you're sleeping in your clothes," Mary June said, putting on lipstick. "If my mother saw you doing that, she'd think you were uncouth."

Kristy lifted her head. "Really?"

Mary June nodded.

"I'll cover myself up, then," said Kristy, as she pulled up the sheet and snuggled in deeper. She yawned. "Don't tell her that I've got my clothes on, okay?"

"Sure, if you want me to lie for you," said Mary June.

Kristy shut her eyes and began to drift off to sleep. The sound of music awakened her.

"Who's playing music?" she asked in a groggy voice. Rolling over to her side, she sat up on her elbow. Mary June was sitting up on her bed, playing her radio.

"Sorry," said Mary June, smiling sweetly. "It's on so softly, I didn't think it would disturb you."

"It's okay," said Kristy, getting out of bed. "Besides, I was thirsty." She got up and headed for the bathroom.

Kristy splashed her face at the sink and drank a cool glass of water.

"Want a chocolate bar?" Mary June asked, appearing in the doorway. "That'll keep you up."

"I don't want to be kept up," Kristy said, brushing past her. "I have to sleep before I swim again."

"For the whole afternoon?" asked Mary June.

Kristy nodded.

"Says who?" asked Mary June.

"Says Kirk," replied Kristy, sitting down on her bed. "If I mess up again tonight, my brother will kill me."

"I'm glad I don't have a brother," said Mary June. "I would hate to be bossed around like Kirk bosses you. He doesn't even trust you to manage your own time." She looked at her watch. "You have four whole hours until you have to swim."

"Four hours is a long time," Kristy agreed. "I guess I don't need to sleep for all of it."

"Let's talk for a minute, then," said Mary June. "I promise I won't bother you again after that."

Kristy folded her hands under her head. "I'm wide awake now. So what do you want to talk about?"

Mary June peered at her. "I'd like you to do me a favor," she said.

Kristy glanced at her. "Yes?"

"Since you had such a bad time this morning, I thought you might not want to be the anchor."

"You mean the anchor in the freestyle relay tomorrow?" Kristy said, sitting up.

Mary June nodded. "I'd be glad to take your place. The anchor is a really important position. The last swimmer in the relay. The whole team depends on you when you're the anchor."

"I know," said Kristy. "I'm really excited about it. It means the coach thinks I'm good."

"But you weren't good this morning," argued Mary June.

"That doesn't mean I won't get better tonight," Kristy said.

"You hope you will," said Mary June. "But there are no guarantees. Face it, Kristy, you barely qualified to swim in this evening's race."

"That—That's because I stayed up too late," Kristy sputtered.

Mary June waltzed over to the mirror and looked at herself. "The anchor should be the best swimmer."

Kristy felt her heart beating fast. "And you think you're the best swimmer?"

"I certainly did better than you did this morning," Mary June said, turning to face her.

"What about last night?" Kristy said.

"Last night didn't count. You were swimming the butterfly," said Mary June. "Do you want the team to win the freestyle relay tomorrow? Or do you want to be responsible for the team losing?"

"Of course I don't want the team to lose," Kristy said.

"Then let me be the anchor," said Mary June. She sat down at the foot of Kristy's bed. "I'm only offering to do it so you won't be embarrassed. I'm only offering to do it because I'm your friend."

"I'll think about it," Kristy said, jumping up.

Mary June smiled. "Okay. Now let's go downstairs and play at the video arcade."

"I don't think I should," said Kristy.

"Oh, please," said Mary June. "Mummy won't let me go without a buddy. And I'm dying to have you teach me The Human Shark."

"It's kind of a stupid game," said Kristy. "Besides, I don't have any money."

"I'll pay for it," said Mary June, grabbing her hand. "We'll be back in plenty of time. Then we can both take a nap."

Kristy stretched. "Okay," she said, looking down at her watch. "I'll play for half an hour. Then I'll come back upstairs and rest."

"Sounds like a good plan," said Mary June. "I'll just tell Mummy."

Kristy combed her hair while Mary June knocked on her mother's door and opened it a crack.

"We're going to the video arcade," Mary June sang out to her mother. "All the other kids are probably going to be there. Okay?"

"I don't know," said Mrs. Williams. "Those games are so addictive."

"All the other mothers are letting their groups go," said Mary June. "Besides, Kristy really wants to play. She can't go by herself. I have to go with her."

Kristy's face got hot. Mary June had explained things backward.

"All right," said Mrs. Williams. "Don't be gone too long."

"Your mother is going to think I'm addicted to video games," Kristy told Mary June when they got into the elevator. "You're the one who said we should go to the arcade, not me."

"But you're the one who stayed there until after one last night," Mary June pointed out. "You're so touchy. What do you care what my mother thinks?"

Downstairs at the arcade, Kristy looked around for the Dolphins, but none of them was there.

"I thought you told your mother that the whole team was coming down," said Kristy.

"I exaggerated," Mary June said, reaching into her purse for quarters. "I had to. Otherwise Mummy wouldn't have let us go."

Kristy looked at The Human Shark and frowned. Playing the game didn't seem so exciting. Somehow being with Mary June was taking the fun out of things.

"Let's play together," said Mary June. "I bet I'll beat you."

"You go ahead," said Kristy. "I'd rather play on my own after you finish."

Mary June smiled. "If that's the way you feel about it. But you can go first. I'll buy us some popcorn." She handed Kristy some money and walked off.

Kristy put some quarters into the slot and grabbed the throttle. As the swimmers started their race, she began to giggle. "This really is the stupidest game," she said, trying to maneuver her swimmer up the lane. Before she got to level two, the human shark jumped over. And at that instant she felt someone tapping on her shoulder. She turned around and saw Kirk.

"You interrupted me," Kristy said. "I was just about to get eaten."

"I thought you were going to rest," Kirk said, scowling.

"I can manage my own time," said Kristy. "I have plenty of time to take a nap."

"Maybe you should have taken a nap first," said Kirk.

"I tried to," Kristy argued. "But I couldn't sleep. You should stop bossing me so much. You're not Mom or Dad."

"It's a good thing Mom and Dad aren't here," Kirk said, shaking his head. "They'd really be disappointed in how you're acting. Not to mention the fact that you're messing up our reputation as the Nuclear Adams."

"I said I was sorry about this morning," said Kristy.

"It's not the way you swam I'm talking about," said Kirk. "I'm talking about the way you're behaving. I ran into that reporter just now. He asked me if I liked to play video games as much as you did."

"So?" said Kristy.

"The Nuclear Adams are swimmers," said Kirk, "not video game artists. If that reporter writes about how you stayed up all night playing this stupid game, it'll be pretty embarrassing for both of us."

Tears sprang to Kristy's eyes. "Maybe you should get another sister who's more disciplined. Maybe then you'd be on the perfect brother-and-sister team that all the newspapers want to write about."

Kristy ran through the lobby toward the elevator. Rosa, Jonah, and Donna were coming out.

"Hey, what's wrong?" Rosa called after her.

"I have something in my eye," Kristy said, wiping a tear away. "I've got to rest. I'll talk to you later."

When Kristy got back to the room, Mrs. Williams was nowhere in sight. Kristy threw herself onto her bed and cried. If only she hadn't stayed up the night before. If only Mary June wasn't so weird. One minute she acted as if she was Kristy's friend, and the next she was saying mean things and lying.

"I wish I'd never come to Junior Olympics," Kristy moaned. She sniffed and reached for a tissue. "Well, I'm here now," she said, glimpsing her face in the mirror. "And I might as well make the best of it."

She closed the blinds and pulled off her shoes, then curled up in bed. She put a pillow over her ears, in case Mary June came back. Then, closing her eyes, she instantly fell asleep.


"Kristy, wake up." Mrs. Williams nudged her gently. "You have a telephone call."

Kristy blinked. "How long have I been sleeping?"

"I'm not sure," said Mrs. Williams. "But your mom's on the phone. Where's Peaches?"

"Downstairs in the video arcade," said Kristy.

She grabbed the telephone. "Mom?"

"Hi, sweetheart. I just wanted to see how you're doing."

Kristy sighed. "It's great to hear your voice," she said.

"You don't sound great," said Dr. Adams. "Anything bothering you?"

Kristy twirled a piece of her hair. "I didn't swim too well today."

"That's too bad," said Dr. Adams. "But you're swimming this evening, aren't you?"

"Yes," said Kristy.

"Then you've got another chance," her mother said in a soothing voice. "Just do the best you can."

"I will, Mom," said Kristy. "I . . . miss you."

"I miss you too, sweetheart," said Dr. Adams. "Good luck tonight. Dad and I will be rooting for you. I'll see you tomorrow. Don't forget that swimming is supposed to be fun."

"I won't forget, Mom."

When Kristy hung up the phone, she felt better. As usual, her mother had said just the right thing. Kristy opened up the blinds and packed her team suit, cap, and goggles neatly. Then she went into the bathroom and carefully shaved her legs.

* * *

"Thanks a lot," said Mary June. The girls were back at the college pool, changing in the locker room.

"Thanks for what?" Kristy asked.

"Thanks for telling my mother I was playing video games all afternoon."

Kristy pulled on her cap.

"She came down to the arcade and practically dragged me away by my hair," Mary June said.

"I couldn't lie and say you were somewhere else," Kristy said.

"You didn't care so much about lying when we stuffed our beds with pillows," said Mary June, angrily pushing her hair into her swim cap.

"Stuffing the pillows was your idea," Kristy reminded her.

"You're right," Mary June said sweetly. "I'm sorry."

Perching on the side of the dressing table, she stared at Kristy. "Have you thought any more about letting me take your place as anchor?"

"I can only think about tonight's race right now," Kristy said, finally looking into Mary June's eyes. "I'll think about tomorrow's race tomorrow. Right now I'm just going to have fun."

Kristy tossed a towel around her shoulders and

started toward the door. Just before she left, she turned back. "Good luck," she called out to Mary June.

"Thanks," said Mary June. "But what makes you think I need it?"

Out in the Dolphins' section, Kristy went straight up to Rosa.

"I filled your water bottle for you," said Rosa.

Kristy grinned and patted Rosa's arm. "You're the best. Have you seen Kirk?" she asked, glancing around.

"He's doing a warm-up lap in the big pool," Rosa said, pointing. "He and Jonah are both swimming the fifty-yard butterfly tonight."

"I know," said Kristy, heading toward the edge of the pool where Kirk was lifting himself out.

"Hey," he said, waving at her.

"Hey yourself," she said, tossing him her towel. "Just wanted to say good luck."

Kirk smiled at her. "You too, sis. I'm . . . I'm sorry I was such a jerk today."

Kristy wrinkled her nose. "You were?"

Kirk shook his head. "I can't believe you didn't notice. I was way out of line telling you what to do with your time."

"Don't worry about it," said Kristy. "It got me to rest."

"How do you feel?" Kirk asked, reaching down for his water bottle.

Kristy took a deep breath. "Okay. I might not do that great tonight," she said. "If I don't, I hope you won't be disappointed. I'm just going to concentrate on enjoying what I'm here to do."

"Sounds good to me," Kirk said, taking a swig of water. He touched Kristy's arm. "All that stuff about the newspaper reporter—I hope you forget it. I'd rather have you as my sister than be called a Nuclear Adams any day."

Kristy giggled. "Thanks. Anyway, you're stuck with me."

Coach Reich walked up to them.

"Take your places in the section," he said. "The meet is about to begin. Have fun, you two."

"We will, Coach," said Kristy.

Settling down on their sleeping bags, Kirk and Kristy watched the beginning of the meet. The first event was the eight-year-old boys' twenty-five-yard freestyle. Kristy smiled as the eight little boys lined up in front of their lanes.

"They look so cute and small," she said.

"Six more years and they'll look like me," Kirk said, flexing his muscles.

Kristy shook her head. "If you weren't my brother, I'd say you were conceited."

The beeper went off, and the little boys dove into the pool. A chubby, dark-haired boy, much faster than all the others, came in first, without his goggles. An official with a net fished the goggles out of the pool.

Kirk laughed. "I lost my goggles when I was his age."

"You lost your goggles last month," Jonah said, walking up. He tapped Kirk on the shoulder. "We're next," he said with a grin. "This time I'm coming in first."

"We'll see about that," Kirk said. He and Jonah slapped hands. "Tell you what—whoever comes in first has to buy the Cokes."

"It's a deal," said Jonah.

Kristy watched her brother and his friend go off to their lanes as the official announced the fourteen-year-old men's fifty-yard butterfly. Her body tensed as Kirk held his position and the beeper went off.

"Look at them go," Rosa said, sitting down next to Kristy. "I wish I could qualify for J.O. someday. But I'm such a slow swimmer."

"Just keep practicing," Kristy said, following Kirk and Jonah with her eyes.

"It's funny," said Rosa. "Watching Kirk and Jonah swimming, it's almost like I'm swimming myself."

"I know what you mean," Kristy said. Her head turned as the swimmers changed direction. "When you watch a sport, you don't just watch with your eyes. You watch with your body."

Kristy stood up as the swimmers came in. Kirk was second, and Jonah was third.

"Great race!" Rosa said, applauding.

"Poor Jonah," said Kristy. "He's always just behind Kirk."

"I know," said Rosa. "But he seems to be a good sport about it."

Kristy waved in Kirk's direction.

"Your event is next," Rosa reminded her.

"I know," Kristy said, taking a deep breath.

As she headed toward the pool, she passed her brother. "Nice going," she said. Kirk's eyes were red from the chlorine.

"Thanks," he said. "Knock 'em dead."

Kristy had been assigned to lane two. Brushing by without speaking, Mary June took the center lane. Kristy remembered what Mary June had said about not needing luck.

Kristy looked at the pool stretching out in front of her. After her poor time that morning, she certainly wasn't as confident as Mary June. She remembered what her mother had said about enjoying herself, and her shoulders relaxed. *I can only do my best,* she told herself.

The beeper went off. Kristy made a perfect dive. A wave of excitement went through her as she entered the water, and adrenaline kept her going. She swam the first lap in a steady rhythm, then pushed herself just at the right moment. Touching the wall for the final time, she looked up at the clock and saw that she'd come in third.

*I came in third!* she thought, climbing out of the pool. *I came in third!*

The timer shook her hand and gave her the card with her time written on it. Kristy felt warm all over.

"Nice job," Coach Reich said. He shook her hand and walked quickly toward the center lane of the pool, where there was some sort of commotion. Kristy watched in amazement. Mary June was just coming in, holding her leg. An official was helping her out. Mrs. Williams ran onto the deck.

"What happened, Peaches?" Kristy heard Mrs. Williams say.

"I got a cramp," Mary June answered loudly. Her face was one big scowl. "I got a cramp. Or I would have come in first."

# EIGHT

"What a comeback!" Kirk said, putting an arm around Kristy in the elevator. Kristy held tight to her medal. "I knew you could do it, sis."

"Thanks," said Kristy. She looked through the walls of the glass elevator and down into the lobby. "I wonder how Mary June is," she said. "Mrs. Williams told me to get on the bus without them."

"They had a taxi drive them back to the hotel," Rosa said, peeking out from behind Kirk's shoulder.

"It was a really rough break," said Jonah. "She was swimming hard."

"She wasn't the only one swimming hard tonight," Donna said with a grin. She tapped Jonah's arm. "You and Kirk brought in another silver and a bronze."

Kirk and Jonah slapped hands and clicked their medals together.

On the thirtieth floor the Dolphins piled out. "Would you like me to walk you to your room, Kristy?" asked Donna's mother. "Just in case Mrs. Williams isn't there yet."

"No thanks," Kristy said, walking away. "I'll just go check the room and see you later."

"We're going for pizza," Rosa said. "Come knock on our door."

Fishing around in her gym bag, Kristy took out her room key. As she was about to open the door, she heard the voices of Mary June and her mother.

"I did my best, Mummy," Mary June was saying. "I can't help it if I got a cramp."

"I'd like to know the reason why," said Mrs. Williams. "Hadn't you warmed up properly?"

"Yes," Mary June whined. "People get cramps. Things like that happen. I would have come in first if I hadn't."

"What a shame," Mrs. Williams said with a sigh. "This will be your first Junior Olympics without at least a silver medal."

Kristy knocked on the door and then slid her key into the slot. Mrs. Williams met her right away.

"Be very quiet," she told Kristy. "Mary June is resting. Of course she should have rested this afternoon. But she insisted on going with you to play video games."

Kristy tiptoed in and put down her things. Mrs. Williams followed her every move.

"Congratulations on your bronze medal," Mary June's mother said crisply. "With the amount of sleep you got last night, I can't imagine how you did it."

Kristy gulped. "I took a nap this afternoon."

"I wish you'd brought Mary June up to take a nap too," Mrs. Williams muttered. Shaking her head, she opened her door. "Maybe if she'd been more rested, her leg wouldn't have cramped."

Mrs. Williams shut the door of her room quietly. Kristy sat down on her bed. Mary June was lying with her eyes open, staring at the ceiling.

"Does your leg still hurt?" Kristy asked.

"Of course not," snapped Mary June. "A cramp only lasts for a couple of minutes."

"I'm glad of that," Kristy said.

Mary June made a sour face. "I'm sure you *are* glad. If it hadn't been for my cramp, you wouldn't have a medal."

"That's not true," Kristy said, holding the medal more tightly.

Mary June sighed and turned over on her pillow. "Can I see it?" she asked, sitting up on her elbow.

Kristy gave Mary June the medal. The bronze shone warmly in the late-afternoon sun flooding through the window.

"You can have it back," Mary June said, tossing the medal by its ribbon. "It's only a bronze anyway. I have one too."

Kristy put the medal on the dresser. "Want to go for pizza?" she asked.

"Fat chance that my mother will let me go," said Mary June.

"Well, maybe you should rest," Kristy suggested. "Do you think you'll be able to swim tomorrow?"

"Of course I will," Mary June said, getting up out of bed. "I didn't *break* my leg. Not that swimming tomorrow will do me any good."

"What do you mean?" asked Kristy, turning around. "Tomorrow's the relay. That's the most exciting part of the meet."

Mary June's eyes teared up. "And you get to bring in the glory. Because you're the anchor."

Kristy sat down in the armchair. "Don't cry," she said. "The relay is for the team. The anchor isn't the only one swimming. There are going to be four of us."

"The anchor is still the glory spot," Mary June insisted. She cried some more and grabbed a tissue. "You said you'd think about letting me take your place."

"But I—I don't need you to take my place," Kristy stammered. "This morning I was off, but this afternoon I swam okay. I feel fine. I don't need a substitute."

"I'm not asking you to scratch," Mary June said. Her eyes bored into Kristy. "I'm asking you to switch places with me so that I can bring in the trophy. I'm faster than you at the freestyle and you know it."

Kristy's heart pounded in her ears. She clenched her fists. "You're really being mean. I think you're just jealous."

Mary June started to cry again. "I'm sorry. I have to win something big, don't you understand? I want to bring in that trophy tomorrow morning for the team. Please, Kristy. Let me do it."

Mrs. Williams opened the door. Mary June wiped her eyes.

"What's going on in here?" Mary June's mother said, shutting the blinds. "Why are you upset, Peaches?" Hurrying to Mary June's side, Mrs. Williams shot a sharp glance at Kristy.

"No reason," Mary June said gloomily. "Just that I'm disappointed because in tomorrow morning's relay I'm not the anchor."

Mrs. Williams stroked Mary June's hair. "Poor thing," she said.

Kristy bolted for the door.

"Where are you going?" asked Mrs. Williams.

"For pizza with Rosa," said Kristy. "Is that okay? Mrs. O'Brien and Donna will be there."

"Of course," said Mrs. Williams. "That'll give Mary June a little time to calm down. See you later, Kristy."

Kristy ran down the hall toward Rosa and Donna's room. The two girls were coming out with Donna's mother.

"What's wrong?" asked Rosa. "You look weird."

"Mary June is very upset," said Kristy.

"Because of her leg cramp?" asked Donna.

"Not exactly," said Kristy. "She's mad at me because she wants to be anchor."

"Naturally she would be," said Rosa. "Mary June can't stand to see someone else win."

"But in the relay the whole team will be winning," Kristy protested.

"The anchor is usually the strongest swimmer," Donna said. "Mary June can't stand the fact that Coach Reich chose you."

"I do think it's the coach's business to decide, though," Mrs. O'Brien said. She squeezed Kristy's shoulder. "Coach Reich has been around for a while. He knows best."

Downstairs the girls made a beeline for the pizza parlor and buried their heads in the menus. Five minutes later Kirk and Jonah walked in with Mr. Walsh.

"Hey, Kriss," Kirk said. He gave Kristy's ponytail a little tug. "Coach Reich is out in the lobby next to the fountain. He wants to see you."

"Sure," said Kristy. "Order me two slices with everything on it but anchovies," she told Rosa.

Out in the lobby, Kristy spotted Coach Reich. The coach smiled and waved Kristy over.

"Congratulations on your excellent time this afternoon," the coach said. He extended his hand to Kristy, and she shook it.

"Thanks, Coach."

The coach motioned to her to sit down.

"I heard about what happened last night," he said, scratching his head. "Now I understand what happened to you in the preliminaries this morning. You must have been exhausted."

Kristy felt her neck get hot. "You know about last night?"

"Mrs. Williams caught me just as I was leaving my room to come down here," he said. "I'm surprised at that stunt you pulled with the pillows."

"I . . . I guess it was pretty sneaky," Kristy said.

"It certainly was. Don't do it again," he warned.

Kristy hung her head. "I won't."

The coach cleared his throat. "Mrs. Williams is convinced that the reason Mary June had a cramp today is that you were a bad influence. That you got Mary June into playing video games instead of resting."

"That's not true," Kristy blurted out.

"Well, I know the part about the cramp is rubbish," the coach agreed. "You play video games with your fingers, not with your legs."

Kristy smiled weakly.

"But sneaking away from your chaperone and deliberately disregarding my training instructions—well, those are serious violations," said the coach.

"I'm really sorry," said Kristy.

"Pretty clever idea, stuffing the bed with pillows," the coach said, cocking his head. "Did you think of that yourself?"

"No," Kristy said quietly.

"Want to tell me about it?" the coach asked. "There's more than one side to a story. I know that."

Kristy thought for a moment. "It wasn't my idea to sneak out," she said, "but I did it. And I stayed up playing video games because I wanted to. Nobody made me do it. I'm sorry."

Coach Reich stood up. "Thanks for taking responsibility for your actions, Kristy. Since I've never had any trouble from you before, we'll shelve this incident for the moment. Let's just say you're on probation for now. Meanwhile, maybe you'd like to bunk in with Donna O'Brien and Rosa Gonzalez tonight. I can arrange for the management to bring in a cot."

Kristy's face lit up. "Oh, could I?"

"I think it would be best for everyone," said the coach. He touched Kristy's shoulder. "We all make mistakes, Kristy. It's important that we learn from them. Now, have a good swim tomorrow. The team's depending on you."

"I won't let them down," said Kristy.

Later that night in Rosa and Donna's room, Kristy snuggled into her cot.

"Is Mary June going to swim tomorrow?" asked Donna.

"As far as I know," said Kristy. "I feel kind of sorry for her."

"How can you feel sorry for her?" asked Donna. "She's so conceited."

"Winning's the most important thing in the world to her," said Kristy. "It seems to be important to her mom, too."

"No one wins all the time," said Rosa.

"Come to think of it," said Donna, "Mary June must be pretty unhappy."

"I think she is," said Kristy.

Mrs. O'Brien came into the room. "You girls get some rest," she whispered.

"Sure, Mom," said Donna, reaching over to turn off the light.

Mrs. O'Brien tucked each of them in. "You look so thoughtful, Kristy," she said.

"I'm thinking about my mom and dad," Kristy said. "I kind of miss them."

"Certainly you do," said Mrs. O'Brien. She straightened Kristy's top sheet. "Tomorrow is the final day. You'll see them soon."

A gentle hush fell over the room. Soon Kristy heard light snoring.

Rosa giggled.

"Donna says you snore too," Kristy whispered back.

"I don't believe it," said Rosa. "You'll have to tell me in the morning if I do."

"I won't be able to," Kristy said, yawning. "I'll be asleep before you."

"Hey, Kristy."

"Yes?"

"Are you and Mary June still friends?"

"I'm not sure," Kristy whispered. "Sometimes she's nice, but then she's mean. Then again, she always says she's sorry. I like being friends with you better. It's less complicated."

"Me too," said Rosa. "Good night."

"Good night," Kristy sighed, already drifting off. She could hardly wait for the next day.

# NINE

"This is probably the only restaurant in the world that serves pasta for breakfast," remarked Mrs. O'Brien as Kristy, Rosa, and Donna plowed into their plates of lasagna.

"They have to serve pasta in the morning with so many swimmers here," said Donna. She wiped her mouth and took a swallow of juice.

"Even if it is only six o'clock in the morning," Rosa said, stifling a yawn.

"I saw that yawn," said Mrs. O'Brien. "I hope you girls weren't up chatting all night long."

"Don't worry," said Kristy, buttering her roll, "we weren't chatting. We were snoring."

Donna giggled.

Rosa nudged Kristy. "Don't look now," she whispered, "but there's your old roommate."

Across the room, Mary June and Mrs. Williams were taking seats at a booth. Catching Mary June's eye, Kristy waved. Mary June didn't wave back.

"Maybe she's mad because you didn't stay in her room," Rosa said.

"Who knows why she's mad?" Donna said. "She's so moody."

"Finish your breakfast, girls," said Mrs. O'Brien. "Don't waste your time gossiping."

When Kristy, Donna, and Rosa filed out of the restaurant, Kristy waved at Mary June again. But Mary June pretended not to see her. The same thing happened on the bus. In the locker room at the pool, Kristy finally went up to Mary June while she was changing.

"Sorry I didn't stay in your room last night," Kristy said. "It was the coach's idea."

"Who cares?" said Mary June. She slammed her goggles down onto the table.

"I didn't mean to hurt your feelings," said Kristy.

Mary June glared. "I said it didn't matter."

"You're mad about something," said Kristy.

Mary June put her hands on her hips. "I'm angry that you're so selfish," she said. "You're putting yourself before the team. If you cared about the team, you'd let me be the anchor in the relay."

"You're the one who's being selfish," Kristy said. "The only reason you want to be the anchor is so that if the team wins, you can hold up the trophy."

"That's not true," Mary June said, stamping her foot. "The reason I want to be the anchor is that I'm the fastest swimmer in freestyle and I'm a more experienced swimmer than you."

Kristy thought for a minute. "You are more consistent than I am," she said. "But if the coach wants me to be anchor, it's because he knows he can depend on me. If he didn't think I was the right person for the spot, he wouldn't give me the chance." She stuck out her chin stubbornly. "All I can do is my best."

"Let's hope your best is good enough," Mary June said, storming away.

Kristy showered and went out to the warm-up pool, where she swam laps with Donna. "I found your water bottle in the locker room," said Rosa as Kristy got out of the pool.

"Thanks," Kristy said, rubbing her face with the towel. "I left in a hurry."

"Want me to do a visualization with you?" Rosa asked, handing Kristy her sweatshirt.

Kristy smiled. "Sounds good. I'd love to get my mind off a certain person who's still mad at me."

"This should help," Rosa said, leading her to a spot on the side of the pool.

Kristy sat down and hugged her knees to her chest.

"Ready?" Rosa asked, kneeling beside her.

"Fire away," Kristy said, shutting her eyes.

"See yourself walking up to the big pool," Rosa said. "You're taking your place for the relay. You feel relaxed and excited."

Kristy opened one eye. "You're good at this. That's just the way I feel."

"You look out at the rest of the team and Coach Reich. Everyone is smiling. Then you look out into the stands and there's your mom. She's calling 'Good luck!' and waving to you."

Kristy imagined seeing her mother and father. It made her feel good.

"Now see yourself swimming the best you've ever swum," said Rosa. "The race is over. You've won."

Kristy kept her eyes shut while the pleasant images washed over her.

"You should be a hypnotist," she said at last, opening her eyes.

"Thanks," said Rosa. "I'm thinking of going into sports psychology."

"I thought you were interested in sports medicine," Kristy said, getting up.

"They're pretty connected," said Rosa. "After all, when we do physical things, it affects the way we feel and think."

"You're right," said Kristy. "After I swim, my

thoughts are usually much clearer and I have a lot of energy."

"Not only that," said Rosa, "you can use your thoughts to prepare yourself better for doing athletic things."

"Like we did just now," said Kristy.

"Hey, Kriss," Kirk said, walking up to them. "You'd better get out to the big pool."

"Why?" asked Kristy. "There's plenty of time yet."

"I just think you ought to get your stuff out to the Dolphins' section, that's all," said Kirk. "Trust me on this."

"Will you ever stop bossing me around?" asked Kristy.

"Tell her she should get out there, Rosa," said Kirk. He touched Rosa's arm, and she smiled. "I'm her big brother. And I know best." He winked at her.

"Maybe you should go out," Rosa told Kristy, trying to read Kirk's expression.

"Fine," said Kristy, "I'm outnumbered." She retrieved her gym bag, water bottle, and towels. "Are you coming?" she asked her brother.

"In a minute," Kirk said, leaning in closer to Rosa. As Kristy passed through the archway to the big pool, she glanced back at them. Kirk was whispering into

Rosa's ear, and Rosa was grinning widely. "Guess he just wanted to get rid of me," she muttered.

Depositing her things in the Dolphins' section, she leaned against the wall and stretched out her hamstrings. Then she felt a gentle touch on her back. Turning slowly, she found herself face to face with her mother.

"Mom!" she cried. "What are you doing here?"

Dr. Adams gave Kristy a tight hug. "I got in very late last night," she said. "You left the hotel so early this morning, I missed you there. I just saw Kirk."

Kristy laughed. "That's why he was acting so mysterious. He wanted me to come out here so that I would bump into you."

"I wanted to surprise you," said Dr. Adams. She touched Kristy on both shoulders. "Is it my imagination, or have you grown in the last three days?"

"Has it only been three days?" asked Kristy. "It feels like three weeks."

"You've packed a lot in," Dr. Adams pointed out. "And you won a bronze medal. I'm sure glad I'm here to catch the tail end of the meet."

"How is Grandma?" Kristy asked, tugging her mother's hand.

Dr. Adams smiled. "Much better. I only wish she could be here. Along with your father, of course."

"Things should be starting up soon," Coach Reich said, walking over to them. He shook Dr. Adams's hand. "Nice to have you here."

"Thanks, Coach," said Dr. Adams.

Kristy and Dr. Adams took seats while Kirk, Jonah, and two other Dolphins took their places for the medley relay. Each boy would swim a different stroke.

"Who does the coach have starting?" Dr. Adams asked.

Kristy pointed to a wiry-looking boy who was removing his glasses. "Oliver Baron," she said. "I saw his name on the lineup when I was coming in."

"Good choice," Kristy's mother commented. "Oliver is a strong backstroker."

"George Martinez will be next, swimming the breaststroke," said Kristy, pointing to a chubby boy with jet black hair.

"Is Kirk swimming the fly?" Dr. Adams asked. "Or is he the anchor?"

"Kirk is swimming the fly. The coach put Jonah in as the anchor, so he'll come in last swimming freestyle," Kristy told her mother.

"Let's keep our fingers crossed that they bring in a victory for the Dolphins," said Dr. Adams.

Kristy crossed her fingers. Her heart began to beat faster. Watching a relay was almost as exciting as swimming in one. She especially liked watching the individual medley relay.

"Which do you like best," Dr. Adams asked, "the medley relay or the freestyle relay?"

"I like watching the I.M.," said Kristy. "But as a swimmer I like to participate in the freestyle. And guess what, Mom? This morning I'll be the anchor!"

Dr. Adams gave her a little hug. "How exciting!"

"Swimmers, get in the water." The loudspeaker boomed through the stadium, and the backstrokers took their positions. Kirk would be the third swimmer, so he had to wait. Standing in place in front of Jonah, he glanced up at the audience. Dr. Adams and Kristy waved. The beeper sounded, and the first swimmers began their strokes.

The audience cheered loudly as the swimmers sprinted for the wall. The instant the first swimmers touched the wall, the second swimmers entered the water. They finished their laps, and the third swimmers started.

Kristy leaned forward. "Come on, Kirk!" she yelled. Her brother's powerful butterfly sent him soaring toward Jonah, the last swimmer.

"Come on, Jonah!" Kristy yelled. She stood up as Jonah took his dive.

Neck and neck with a competing freestyler, Jonah

touched the wall. Kristy looked up at the time board. The Dolphins had come in first by one-hundredth of a second.

"We did it!" Kristy cried, jumping up and down.

"We did it!" Donna shouted behind her.

"Better get ready," Rosa said, tapping Kristy on the shoulder. "Your turn's coming soon."

Riding the wave of the team's victory in the individual medley, Kristy took her place at the pool for the freestyle relay. The coach had assigned the starting position to Donna. Then came Geraldine Johnson, Mary June, and finally Kristy. The four girls paced beside the pool.

"I'm kind of nervous," Donna whispered as she passed Kristy.

"You'll do fine," Kristy whispered back. "Just keep your focus." She swallowed and took a deep breath. It was easy for her to tell Donna not to be nervous, but she was nervous herself. Remembering what Mary June had said about the team's depending so much on the anchor, Kristy felt her knees get wobbly. Then she thought of Kirk and Rosa and of Coach Reich. She looked up at the stands and saw her mother. They all had confidence in her. They all thought she could do it.

*I* can *do it*, she said to herself.

"Swimmers, take your mark." The voice came over

the speaker. Kristy saw Donna start her walk to the block, shaking out her hands. A tense moment later, the beeper went off and Donna and the starting swimmers from the other teams dived in. The swimmers next in line took their places. As Donna finished her swim and touched the wall, Geraldine Johnson expertly arched into the water, and Mary June got into position to jump in. Kristy took a deep breath to calm her racing heart. The Dolphins were in the lead. She heard Kirk yell from the audience, "Come on, Dolphins!"

Geraldine touched the wall. Mary June dived in. Kristy stepped onto the block. Mary June stroked with power and grace, giving the Dolphins an even greater lead. As she turned for her final lap, Kristy got into position for her dive. Every muscle in her body was alert as she held her mark. Keeping her eyes on Mary June, she found an inner calm. Timing was everything in a moment like this. Starting a split second early would disqualify Kristy, and the relay would be lost.

Keeping her focus on Mary June's cap, she leaned out over the water. Suddenly Mary June's pace slacked off. She didn't break stroke, but she wasn't swimming as fast.

*Hurry!* Kristy thought. *Hurry!* The team was losing valuable seconds. Only an instant before, a win for the Dolphins had seemed a sure thing. Now they were losing their lead. Kristy realized she would have to give everything she had to bring the team in first.

*I can do it!* Kristy thought. Mary June touched the wall. Kristy dived into the water and glided forward. She felt a surge of power as her kick pushed her across the pool. Her arms pulled through the water with a strength she'd never experienced. When she touched the wall for the final time, she felt dazzled.

"You did it." Coach Reich's voice broke the spell. For an instant Kristy had been lost. Lost in motion.

She looked up at the cheering crowd as she climbed from the pool. She barely felt Donna's hug.

"I can't believe it," Kristy murmured, breaking into a smile. "We won."

When the team picked up its two trophies at the awards table, Mary June was nowhere to be found.

"Have you seen Mary June?" Coach Reich asked Rosa.

"Mrs. Williams told me Mary June isn't feeling well," Rosa reported. "She had to leave early."

"What a shame," said Coach Reich. "We'll have to take the picture without her."

Holding the freestyle relay trophy, Kristy stood in the front row next to Jonah. Standing on the other side of her, Kirk put an arm around Kristy's shoulder. Dr. Adams took the official picture for the coach.

"Can I get one too?" Charles Flowers asked, strolling up.

"Sure thing," Coach Reich called out. "Stay where you are, Dolphins," he instructed. "I know we all want to get to the beach and celebrate. Just one more photo for *The Surfside Gazette.*"

"Thanks," the reporter said, smiling.

His camera's flash went off.

"Yay, Dolphins!" Kirk shouted. He shook Jonah's hand and stroked the I.M. trophy. "Congratulations, Jonah," he said. "You did it for us."

"We all did it," said Jonah.

"That's right," Kristy said, holding the freestyle trophy in the air. "It was all of us!"

# TEN

Lying on the beach in her new yellow two-piece, Kristy gazed up at a puffy white cloud.

"Isn't it just perfect to have the team party at the beach?" Rosa said, settling her hot pink sunglasses on top of her head. "Look at Kirk and Jonah." She pointed. The two boys were wading into the waves with their surfboards.

"In search of the perfect wave," Kristy said lazily.

Rosa took a sip of ginger ale. The girls' blanket was strewn with an array of chips, cookies, and other party food. "I'm almost ready to jump in the water myself," Rosa announced.

"Not me," Kristy said. She rolled over and reached for the sunblock. "I've been in the water so much lately, I could use a good bake. After Junior Olympics last weekend, I thought the coach would give us a couple of days off. But there we were back in the pool for practice on Monday afternoon. Not to mention the morning practice we had with the school swim team."

Rosa smiled. "Being on two teams must get to be a bit much. But you love it, don't you?"

Kristy grinned. "I'm definitely hooked on swimming."

"Especially now that you've got a bronze medal from Junior Olympics," Rosa said. "I wonder if I'll ever get a medal," she said with a sigh.

"Sure you will," Kristy said, offering her a chip. "You just have to keep at it. Who knows? Maybe someday you and I will have to swim against each other."

Rosa rolled her eyes. "I don't think I could do it. I couldn't compete against my best friend. It would ruin everything."

"No it wouldn't," said Kristy. "A swim meet is over in one day. Friendship lasts forever. It would be silly to be mad at a friend because she does better than you."

"I don't know," said Rosa. "Look what happened to you and Mary June."

"That was different," Kristy said, standing up. She looked down the beach. The Dolphins were everywhere, swimming, playing with Frisbees, or lying on blankets. Kristy's parents were there too, sharing an umbrella with Coach Reich. In a far corner near the ice cream stand, Kristy caught sight of Mary June. She was wearing a floppy sun hat and sitting with her mother.

"Mary June was never really my friend, even though

she said she wanted to be," Kristy said. "A friend could never have been as spiteful as she was at Junior Olympics."

"You mean the way she was lying?" asked Rosa.

"Yes," Kristy said. "And she did something else." She looked down and kicked the sand at her feet.

"What did she do?" asked Rosa.

"I don't have proof," Kristy said, looking up, "but I think that in the relay she slowed up on purpose."

"I think she did too," said Rosa. "I was watching her."

"She was so angry that she wasn't the anchor, she was willing to sacrifice the team. She was willing to do anything to make sure that I didn't swim the winning lap."

Rosa shook her head. "That's taking competition a little too far. That's really rotten."

"I wonder if Mary June feels rotten about it," Kristy said. "I know I would."

Rosa shrugged and glanced down the beach. "Maybe Mary June doesn't feel rotten at all about what she tried to do. If she feels rotten about anything, it's that she didn't get more glory."

"I kind of feel sorry for her," Kristy said, looking away. "Her mother is so hard on her. And acting the way she does must take the fun out of swimming. Anybody would think that instead of competing at a sport, Mary June was acting out that video game, The Human Shark."

"Come on," Rosa said, grabbing Kristy's hand. "I feel like running."

The girls ran along the edge of the water in the wet sand. Kirk was coasting in on a wave, followed by Jonah.

"The waves are great!" Kirk shouted, lifting his board out of the surf. "Come on in, Rosa. You can borrow my board."

"Borrow *my* surfboard," Jonah called with a laugh, "it's better."

"Maybe later," Rosa called back. "After I finish my run."

Kristy kept running at the edge of the water. Foam trickled over her feet. "Those two compete in everything," she said. "And they're still friends."

Rosa's face dimpled into a smile. "I like them," she said. "Both of them."

Kristy stopped and caught her breath. "Which one do you like better?"

"I don't know," said Rosa. She sat down and picked up a stick. "Which do you think looks best with *R.G.*?" she asked, scratching initials in the sand. "*K.A.* or *J.W.*?"

Kristy kicked the sand playfully. "How should I know? I've never even liked a boy. Let alone been in love."

"It happens to lots of girls," Rosa warned. "It'll happen to you someday."

Kirk ran down the beach, waving a paper. "Hey, Kriss!" he called. "Look what Coach Reich gave to Mom!" Almost bumping into her, Kirk thrust the paper he was holding into her face.

"Oh, no," Kristy groaned. "It's the newspaper."

"Is there something about the Dolphins in there?" Rosa asked.

"Yes," said Kirk. "An article about how the team did at Junior Olympics. There's a whole paragraph about Kristy. And about me," he added, flexing his muscles.

"I don't want to look at it," Kristy said, turning her back. "They probably called me a mackerel."

"Not at all," Rosa said, scanning the article. "Look."

### DOLPHINS BRING
### HOME MEDALS

Commentary by Charles Flowers

Members of the Aquatic Dolphins performed admirably at the Junior Olympics last weekend.

Outstanding were Jonah Walsh, who

brought home two bronze medals, and Mary June Williams, who brought home a bronze. But the stars remained the sensational "Nuclear Adams"—Kirk and Kristy Adams.

Kirk has two silver medals to add to his collection in the 200-yard back and 50-yard butterfly. Though her performance was uneven, Kristy Adams won a bronze in the 50-yard freestyle Saturday night and went on to swim the final winning lap in the freestyle relay Sunday.

These performances in the Junior Olympics represent months of dedicated training and expert coaching by Coach Brian Reich. But the event wasn't all work and no play. The trip provided players an exciting opportunity to socialize with one another and with players from other teams. Kristy Adams even enjoyed a few video games. Just goes to show that a winning swimmer can also be a normal kid.

"Hmm," said Kristy, tapping her foot. "He called me normal."

"Isn't that what you wanted him to say about you?" asked Rosa.

" 'Normal' makes me sound boring," said Kristy.

"How do you think I feel?" Kirk said. "He didn't say anything much about me. And I'm a supersensational athlete."

"And so modest," Rosa said, rolling her eyes.

"I'm the better half of the Nuclear Adams," Kirk argued.

"Better be careful," Kristy teased, "your competitive nature is showing."

"Just kidding, sis," Kirk said, giving her a hug. "It's a nice article. Congratulations."

Kristy looked at her brother and then at Rosa.

"I can't believe I'm saying this. But I'm ready for a swim."

"Let's play Human Shark!" Rosa screeched, splashing out. Kristy and Kirk plunged into the waves after her.

As the surf washed over Kristy's back, her face broke into a smile. She couldn't believe how nutty that reporter was who had written about her. One week he called her a shark and then the next he said she was normal. *Maybe he's right,* she thought. *Maybe I'm both things.* After all, sharks were great swimmers, and hardly any of them were really dangerous. As for the normal part, Kristy couldn't deny that most things in her life were pretty usual—even if Kirk wanted to believe that just because that reporter called them the Nuclear Adams, they were stars.

Ducking under a wave, Kristy came back up stroking. Figuring out whether she was a shark or just normal was complicated. She flipped onto her back and floated. One thing she knew for certain—there was nothing she loved more than the water.

## ABOUT THE AUTHOR

SHARON DENNIS WYETH has written many books for young readers, including *Vampire Bugs: Stories Conjured from the Past, The World of Daughter McGuire,* and the Pen Pals series. She lives in Montclair, New Jersey, with her husband, Sims, and daughter, Georgia.

# Fin Notes

## GETTING MOTIVATED

Excellence in swimming, as in any sport, requires discipline and effort. How do athletes motivate themselves? Here are some people and things that motivate athletes. List them in their order of importance to you. Put the most important motivator first on your list. Put the least important last. Then look at the bottom of the next page to find out how two Olympic swim teams ranked the same items.

| | | |
|---|---|---|
| Friends | Standard Times | Opponents |
| Parents | Self | Awards |
| Records | Teammates | Coach |

# BRAIN TEASERS

How well do you know your swimming history? Check your answers below.

1. What male swimmer set the 100-meter butterfly world record in Orlando at the World Trials in 1992?

2. What female swimmer won the 400-meter freestyle Olympic gold in 1988?

Reference for "Fin Notes": "Swimmer's Handbook" published by United States Swimming

## BRAIN TEASERS

1. Pablo Morales with a time of 52.84.
2. Janet Evans with a time of 4:03.85.

## GETTING MOTIVATED

| | | |
|---|---|---|
| 1. Self | 4. Teammates | 7. Standard Times |
| 2. Coach | 5. Parents | 8. Awards |
| 3. Opponents | 6. Friends | 9. Records |

Don't miss the next exciting adventure of the

*Splash Party*
**American Gold Swimmers #3**

Kirk Adams is thrilled when he gets a job as a life-guard's assistant at a private club in Surfside, Florida. But soon the fourteen-year-old finds out that the job isn't all suntan lotion and bikinis. In fact, it's little more than mopping the deck and blowing up floats at the kiddie pool. To make things worse, his boss is a pretty fifteen-year-old girl who won't give Kirk a second look. Then Kirk's little sister gets a job as a swimsuit model in a TV commercial that will be shot at the club.

Can Kirk keep Kristy from discovering that he's just a glorified baby-sitter?